# ABBY THE BAD SPORT

# ABBY THE BAD SPORT

# Ann M. Martin

AN
**APPLE**
PAPERBACK

SCHOLASTIC INC.
New York Toronto London Auckland Sydney

Cover art by Hodges Soileau

ISBN 0-590-05988-2

12 11 10 9 8 7 6 5 4 3 2 1          7 8 9/9 0 1 2/0

Printed in the U.S.A.                               40

First Scholastic printing, August 1997

*The author gratefully acknowledges*
*Nola Thacker*
*for her help in*
*preparing this manuscript.*

# CHAPTER 1

Was I late?

Not by my watch.

Was I on time? Well, that was another story — and why I was running at full speed toward Claudia Kishi's house at 58 Bradford Court in Stoneybrook, Connecticut, at approximately 5:29 P.M. Give or take a minute.

Except that Kristy Thomas, our fearless leader and president of the Baby-sitters Club (or BSC), does not give minutes away. When she convenes a meeting of the BSC, she calls it to order ON TIME. And she expects everybody to be there.

Everybody including me, even though I would have had a perfectly good excuse to be late and even though I had a million things to do and to catch up on before I . . .

But wait. I guess I'm running ahead of myself. (That's a joke, in case you didn't notice.)

I'm Abby. Abigail Stevenson, to be exact. I

am thirteen years old and in eighth grade at Stoneybrook Middle School in Stoneybrook, Connecticut, where I am an okay student and an *excellent* varsity soccer player. I'm not bragging. I just don't believe in pretending not to be good at something when you are. It's just as dumb as pretending to know how to do something when you don't.

I'm medium-sized (the best size for a soccer player, in my opinion) with dark brown curly hair and brown eyes. I have a soccer tan almost year-round. I am nearsighted and wear glasses (regular and sports glasses) or contacts, depending on my mood. I'm also in top physical shape, except for one little problem.

Life makes me sneeze. Translation: I am ALLERGIC. To everything. Well, maybe not to everything, because I haven't come in contact with everything in the world yet. But I am allergic to dogs, dust, kitty litter (but, amazingly, not cats!), tomatoes, shellfish, cheese, milk, and pollen, big-time. Just to name a few items.

I also have asthma and have to carry an inhaler at all times in case I have an asthma attack. In fact, I have two inhalers, a regular over-the-counter one for when I get a little short of breath and a prescription one for when I have a really bad asthma attack, the kind with big emergency-room-visit potential. (Hospital-level attacks have only happened to me a few times, luckily.)

But enough about asthma and allergies. We — my mother; my twin sister, Anna; and I — moved here recently from Long Island to a bigger house in a kid-friendly neighborhood when my mother got a new publishing job in New York City. Life was supposed to get easier.

Easier was not the word that came to mind when I contemplated moving from the house where we had lived for as long as I could remember. For one thing, I was the star forward, co-captain, and leading scorer on my school's soccer team. I had friends. Some of our relatives lived nearby. And, well, the truth is that the worst part was leaving the house we'd been living in when my dad was killed in an automobile accident four years ago. A truck crashed into my father's car. The driver of the truck was barely even hurt.

Somehow, I thought leaving the house meant we were leaving the memory of my father behind.

But it wasn't true. In fact, it turned out to be just the opposite, because during the move, Anna and I found a box of our father's things that our mother had packed away right after he died. We hardly ever talk about what happened, but when we showed Mom the box, well — we talked.

After that, things between Mom and me and Anna were better.

Anyway, now we live here and I've made new friends, secured my rightful place on the soccer team, become the co-coach of a kids' softball team, and become a successful businesswoman. That last part is where the BSC comes in.

What is the BSC? You mean you haven't heard of us? We're famous all over Stoneybrook!

Actually, kidding aside, we are pretty well-known. But more about that later.

The only thing you need to know about the BSC right now is that it meets Mondays, Wednesdays, and Fridays at Claudia Kishi's (Claudia is the vice-president) at five-thirty P.M. *sharp*.

Which is a mild word for the look Madame President Kristy would give me if I were late.

I flew past Claudia's sister, Janine, with a breathless "Hi — late" when I entered the house. I took the stairs two at a time. I flung open the door of Claudia's room with such force it banged against the wall.

Kristy looked up from the director's chair she commandeers at every meeting. She raised the visor that is her BSC crown, glanced over at the clock as it changed to 5:30, and said, "This meeting of the BSC will come to order."

Yippee. I wasn't late.

I slid down the side of Claudia's bed and gasped, "Water. Give me water."

"How about orange juice mixed with seltzer?" asked Stacey McGill, who is our treasurer. "I have to mix them because the orange juice would be too much sugar for me otherwise."

"Done," I said gratefully.

After I had slaked my thirst and Kristy had fielded a couple of phone calls for baby-sitting jobs, she looked at me and said, "Well, Abby, we're glad you could make it."

"Me too," I said. I meant it. I like the meetings. My closest friends in Stoneybrook are my fellow BSC members.

"How did the training go?" asked Mary Anne, looking up from the record book she keeps as secretary of the BSC. "Is it really only for one day?"

I nodded and Mary Anne made a note in the book.

"Are you free to take on more baby-sitting jobs, then? You know August is a busy month for us," she said. "How many days will practice and games take up?"

"I don't know exactly, but of course I'm free to take jobs. On a case-by-case basis," I said loftily.

Kristy snorted and Mary Anne looked at me

5

quizzically. Mallory Pike said to Jessi Ramsey in a loud whisper that was meant to be heard, "Wow, Abby must be *way* important now to be so busy."

I grinned. "Okay, okay," I said. "This is the deal. Remember when my soccer coach recommended me for the Special Olympics Unified Team program after I said I wanted to get more soccer practice?"

"Yeah, that's what the girl needs," said Claudia to no one in particular. "More soccer."

I ignored her. "Well, lots of kids from several schools have been recommended, both as partners and as athletes."

"Partners and athletes?" asked Mallory, who is one of our junior officers.

"The Unified Teams are made of players who have mental retardation and players who don't," I said. "The players who have mental retardation are referred to as athletes and the players who don't are referred to as partners. Only Coach Wu said — "

"Coach Wu," Kristy interjected. "She's your coach? Wow, are you in for a tough ride. She's good, but she is . . . " Kristy let out a whistle. Kristy had played for Coach Wu on the varsity softball team.

"I like her," I said. "I don't think she can toss out anything I can't handle. Anyway, she said that we are *all* athletes and she's going to expect us to behave accordingly."

I went on to explain that the Special Olympics Unified Teams combine athletes and partners of similar age and athletic skill for training and competition. I also explained that the training was really more of an orientation, so we could ask questions and check things out. "Not everybody on the team will learn or think in the same way or at the same speed," I concluded. "But Stoneybrook United has been set up so that no single player is a superstar, or anything."

I didn't mention that I didn't quite believe this. I'd never played on a team where I wasn't one of the star players. But I had also been very good at helping players who weren't up to my game. Secretly, I kind of thought that was what I would be doing, operating as sort of an assistant coach.

Mallory pushed her glasses into place on the bridge of her nose and said, "Stoneybrook United?"

"Well, there's a great British men's team, Manchester United. And here in the United States the Washington, DC, men's pro team is called DC United. So it seemed only natural, especially since we have players from other schools."

Claudia said cautiously, "It's a good name. But soccer . . . " She let her voice trail off.

I had to laugh. "Think of soccer as a moving art form, Claud. Then you'll like it better. In fact, the really good teams are always moving, making new patterns on the field."

"Geometry," commented Stacey.

"Ick," said Claudia. Then she grinned. "But I like the idea of soccer as a moving art form. Maybe I can come up with some new ideas for a collage I've been thinking about."

"Come to our games," I suggested. "We'll be glad to pose for you."

"I'm going to tell Dawn about it next time I talk to her," said Mary Anne. "I wonder if the Special Olympics has a Unified surfing team?" (Dawn is Mary Anne's stepsister, who lives in California.)

"The Special Olympics Committee sponsors a lot of sports, but I don't think surfing is one of them. Surfing *is* kind of limited to places with beaches. Soccer, on the other hand, is a game you can play anywhere. It's the universal game, the — "

"Abby," said Jessi. "We know."

I stopped and smiled ruefully. I do get a *little* carried away about soccer sometimes.

Then I sighed.

"What's wrong?" asked Mary Anne. Mary Anne is very sensitive and I could see what she was thinking — she was worried that my feelings might have been hurt by what Jessi had said.

"Don't worry," I said. "It's nothing. I just remembered that we are sponsor-free at the moment. The restaurant that was going to sponsor us can't, and we're looking for a new business to back us. But until we find one, or one of us inherits a fortune or finds buried treasure or something, we won't be able to buy team jerseys or new equipment."

Kristy went into her organizational mode. "No jerseys? What about T-shirts? If everybody has a T-shirt that's the same color, you can put numbers on the shirts with tape."

"I know. It's what we're going to do. And it's no big deal." But I couldn't help sighing again. Soccer doesn't require lots of expensive, weird equipment like, say, American football. We could wear homemade shirts and mismatched socks and play just as well as a team in all new duds and with brand-new equipment.

On the other hand, it helps team spirit to look sharp and have decent gear.

Shake it off, I told myself. The important thing is the game, not how you look playing it. "Well, anyway," I said aloud, "Connecticut just happens to have one of the best Unified Sports programs around. And Coach Wu is very cool. Did you know she was varsity at University of

North Carolina at Chapel Hill? And lots of the players on the first U.S. women's Olympic soccer team were from University of North Carolina at Chapel Hill. You know who Mia Hamm is, right? The best player on the 1996 women's soccer team, at least in my opinion. And since the women's team won, that would make her the best player in the world, at least in my opinion. In fact . . . "

"Abby . . . " Mallory said.

I stopped and looked around the room. Mal, Jessi, Mary Anne, Kristy, Stacey, and Claudia were all grinning. Then they said at once, "We know!"

## CHAPTER 2

Not many people could tease me about soccer and live.

Okay, I'm kidding. A little. But my fellow members in the BSC really are among the few people who can tease me about something so important *and* make me laugh about it.

So I guess I'd better fill you in on the Baby-sitters Club.

We're headed by that Master of Organization, Kristy. She thought up the BSC one night while listening to her mother make phone call after phone call trying to find a sitter for Kristy's younger brother, David Michael. Kristy thought, *What if a person could call one number and reach several baby-sitters at once?*

For Kristy, thinking of an idea is almost synonymous with acting on it, so in no time at all the Baby-sitters Club was off and running (or sitting). Kristy, Mary Anne, Claudia, and Stacey were the founding members, but soon the club had more than doubled in size. Now we have seven full-time members, two associate members to handle overflow business, and one long-distance honorary member in California. We don't even have to hand out flyers or put up signs around town anymore, since we have more than enough business from satisfied clients and from people to whom we've been recommended.

As you know, we meet three times a week, in Claudia's room. That's because Claudia is the only member who has her own phone line. Our phone calls during business hours are short and to the point.

We pay dues every Monday. The money is for club expenses, which include the occasional celebratory pizza, gas money for Kristy's brother Charlie, who drives Kristy and me to meetings, and items for the Kid-Kits.

The Kid-Kits are *not* kits from which we assemble children. (Ha-ha.) They are another Kristy brainstorm. We each have a box that we have decorated and filled with kid-friendly things, such as old toys, stickers, crayons and coloring books, games, and puzzles. We don't take the Kid-Kits to every job, but they are a *great* icebreaker when we baby-sit for new clients, or when we sit for kids who are stuck inside because they are sick or because the weather is bad.

In order to keep things organized, we have a record book, in which Mary Anne enters our schedules and all our jobs (she has never, ever made a mistake). We also have a BSC notebook in which we write about every single job we go on. The BSC notebook is a big pain sometimes, because it's a little like homework, but it comes in handy, I'll admit. It helps keep us up-to-date on what's happening with our baby-sitting charges — who's developed a weird dislike of peanut butter, for example, or who's struggling to learn how to ride a bicycle. We can also use it for help in solving baby-sitting problems. Chances are, whatever the situation, one of us has encountered it before and written about it in the notebook.

The BSC is a success because we are organized, reliable, and have good ideas (like the Kid-Kits), and because we are all so very different from one another, in spite of the fact that there are three sets of best friends, plus one couple, in our club.

Take Kristy. Please. (That's a joke. Kristy and I get along fine, but she is *so* stubborn. I mean, she actually argues with *me*!)

You already know that Kristy is our president, the idea queen of the world. In addition to running the BSC, she also coaches Kristy's Krushers, a softball team for kids who are too young or otherwise not ready for Little League (average age of a team member: approximately 5.8 years old). She is also best friends with Mary Anne, even though they couldn't be more different. They are both short, true. Kristy is the shortest person in our class and Mary Anne isn't much taller. They both have brown hair and are members of blended families. They both dress casually, although Mary Anne's style is a little more fashionably preppy.

Kristy is outspoken, opinionated, and, according to some people, pushy. (Isn't it interesting that people call someone who can't be bullied or pushed around pushy?) These are excellent qualities for organizing and running the BSC (and probably the world, someday). They also come in very handy in a large, noisy family. Kristy lives with two older brothers, one younger brother, and, part-time, when they are not living with their mother, one younger stepsister and one younger stepbrother. She also lives with one very young adopted sister, one mother, one stepfather, one grandmother, one dog, one cranky cat, assorted other pets, and, according to a few members of her family, particularly her very imaginative stepsister, Karen, one resident ghost.

Fortunately, Kristy's stepfather, Watson Brewer, is a real, live millionaire (as well as a nice guy, a good cook, and an avid gardener), which is quite a switch from the old days when

Kristy and her mother and brothers had to struggle to make ends meet. When Watson and Kristy's mother got married, the family moved into a real, live mansion. That means plenty of room for everybody, including the ghost.

Mary Anne Spier also comes from a blended family. It is much smaller, however. Mary Anne's mother died when Mary Anne was just a baby. That left Mary Anne's father in charge of her upbringing. He, in turn, was very strict and protective of Mary Anne. That's cool, except that it was hard for Mr. Spier to realize that Mary Anne was growing up. Until recently he made her wear pigtails and even picked out the (little-girl) clothes she wore.

Unlike Kristy, Mary Anne is very quiet and very shy and sensitive (she even cries at sentimental *commercials*). But she *is* as stubborn in her own way as Kristy is. She finally convinced her father that she was old enough to do some things on her own, such as choose her own clothes. When Mr. Spier saw that Mary Anne could handle more responsibility, he relaxed and gave her a little more freedom. She got a kitten, which she named Tigger, and a boyfriend. (You'll hear about him later, since he is an associate member of the BSC.)

Mary Anne also got a whole new stepfamily when her father married his former high school sweetheart — thanks in part to Mary

Anne and her stepsister-to-be, Dawn Schafer. Mary Anne and Dawn had become best friends (yes, Mary Anne has two best friends) shortly after Dawn moved to Stoneybrook from California with her mother and brother after her parents got divorced. Dawn's mother had grown up in Stoneybrook, and when Dawn and Mary Anne discovered the high school sweetheart connection between Mr. Spier and Mrs. Schafer, it seemed only natural to encourage them to get together again.

It worked, wedding bells rang, and Mary Anne and her father (and Tigger) moved in to a cool old farmhouse near the edge of town with Dawn, her mother, and Dawn's younger brother, Jeff. But Jeff decided he missed his father and California too much and went back. Gradually, Dawn also found herself missing her California family. Although it was a very difficult decision, she returned to California too.

Dawn is, as you might have guessed, our honorary California member. Naturally she stays in touch with Mary Anne and her Connecticut family. And recently, Dawn joined the members of the BSC on a cross-country road trip to California.

Another pair of best friends in the BSC are Stacey and Claudia. They are very interested in clothes and fashion. Stacey is always up to the second in her look, while Claudia really likes to push the fashion boundaries.

That's partly because Claudia is an artist. She doesn't like school, but when it comes to being creative, Claudia is every bit as much a genius as her older sister, Janine (who is a real, live genius complete with the I.Q. score to prove it).

Claudia often wears her art on her sleeve — almost literally. On this, my first Monday back at the BSC, for example, she was in a little crop-top muscle shirt that she had batikked green and blue. She'd sewed a bunch of buttons up the front as if it were a vest. She also had on skinny black shorts, one blue sock and one green sock, and black Doc Martens with one blue shoelace (on the foot with the green sock) and one green shoelace (on the foot with the blue sock). Her long black hair had been gathered into a single braid. A blue ribbon with more buttons attached to it was woven into the braid. Her earrings? Buttons, naturally. On anybody else, it might not have — no, it *would* not have — worked. But on Claudia, with her creamy skin, dark brown eyes, and artistic, easy grace, it looked terrific.

Fashion and art aren't the only things Claudia Kishi does well, though. She's also a junk food gourmet, with enough candy, chips, etc. hidden around her room to fuel Halloween.

And she loves Nancy Drew books, which she also keeps hidden since her parents, to her mystification, equate Nancy Drew with junk food.

Junk food is not something you will ever see Stacey McGill eating, however, and not because she's trying to be one of those skinny, icky supermodels. No, Stacey (who is slender, blonde, and much better looking than a starved supermodel, anyway, in my opinion) can't eat sugar. That's because she has diabetes, which means she has to watch what she eats very, very carefully and even give herself insulin injections to make sure that she doesn't get sick.

Stacey never talks about it, but she handles her diabetes with the same self-assurance and efficiency that she handles everything else (including schoolwork, especially math). Maybe that's why she seems older than the other members of the BSC. That — and her New York City fashion sense, which she acquired when she lived in New York before moving to Stoneybrook. Like Dawn, Stacey's parents are divorced. They split up after her father had to move back to New York. Stacey frequently visits him — and brushes up on the latest fashions.

Jessi Ramsey and Mallory Pike are junior members of the BSC, because they are in sixth grade and can't baby-sit at night during the week and only for their families at night on the weekends. They have a shared passion for horses and books about horses, especially the books by Marguerite Henry. But Mallory does not share Jessi's passion for ballet and Jessi does not share Mallory's love of writing stories.

Jessi moved to Stoneybrook from New Jersey with her mother, father, her younger sister, and her baby brother. Her aunt also lives with her family now. Jessi is of medium height, and she's dancer-strong and graceful. She has brown skin and dark brown eyes with dark hair she often wears in a ballet dancer's twist at the nape of her neck. Her fashion taste also reflects her love of ballet. She likes to wear leotards (of which she has a large collection) under sweaters or jackets with jeans or pants.

Jessi is also very disciplined. She gets up every morning at exactly 5:29 to practice ballet at the *barre* her family has set up for her in the basement, and she studies ballet with a special teacher.

Mallory does not get up at 5:29 A.M. every day to write, but she gets up early because she is the oldest of a large family — eight siblings, including a set of triplets. Her vast experience with so many kids is why she was asked to join the BSC. Mallory has reddish hair, pale skin, freckles, and — to her eternal despair —

glasses and braces. She can hardly wait to lose the braces and plans on getting contact lenses as soon as she can.

I think she looks good in glasses and I'm trying to change her mind on that, especially since I wear glasses a lot myself. But so far, I haven't persuaded her.

Whew. Almost done. Our associate members are NOT best friends, but Logan Bruno (this cute guy who resembles the movie star Cam Geary, according to Mary Anne) is Mary Anne's boyfriend. He is into sports in a major way, which I naturally consider a good quality in anybody. He is easygoing and nice and has a trace of a Southern accent, which is not surprising, since he is originally from Kentucky.

Shannon Kilbourne is the only member of the BSC who doesn't go to Stoneybrook Middle School. She goes to a private school, Stoneybrook Day School, along with her two sisters. When she is not in her school uniform, her style runs to casual. She lives across the street from Kristy (and just down from me, since I live two houses over from Kristy). Of all the BSC members, Shannon is probably the most school-achievement-oriented. Check this out. She's a member of the French club, the astronomy club (of which she's the youngest member *and* the vice-president), the Honor Society, and the debate team. And she participates in school plays.

So it is a good thing that BSC associate members don't have to attend meetings, right? Although as organized as Shannon is (she's in Kristy's league on that one), she'd probably manage it somehow.

And that's the BSC.

# CHAPTER 3

Coach Wu blew her whistle. "Okay, everybody, two easy laps to warm up."

Although it was our first practice together, I took it as a good sign that our team did what every team does when it is told to do dull, boring laps. We all groaned.

"And then we stretch," added Coach Wu firmly.

We groaned again, but the coach took no notice. She looked down at her clipboard and began making notes as the members of our team finished lacing up cleats, adjusting shin guards, and peeling off sweats.

"We'll do introductions while we stretch," Coach Wu called as we straggled out onto the field and began to jog slowly around it.

I smiled to myself. I was going to like Coach Wu's style. She didn't waste any time. Then I picked up my speed a little, pounding out my laps at something a little showier than a jog. I figured if the coach was watching, it might impress her. And it doesn't hurt to impress a coach you've never played with before.

Not that I was the only one who was going heads-up around the field. At least two other players were: Petra Kosinski, whom I knew from junior varsity at Stoneybrook Middle School, and another girl I didn't recognize, taller than me and with a ground-eating stride that would strike fear into an unprotected goalie's heart. Petra was a go-getter and I knew she'd be claiming a berth on the varsity team at Stoneybrook pretty soon. If the tall girl's skills matched her stride, she already would have nailed a spot. I didn't recognize her, though. But then, I was fairly new to Stoneybrook.

Hmmm. I won't say that I had a premonition, but . . .

I picked up my pace.

Petra, the tall girl, and I finished at the front of the pack. I peeled off before it could become too obvious that we were working on a race instead of a gentle warm-up jog.

When we had formed a circle around the coach, she began taking us through the warm-up stretches. In between stretches, we introduced ourselves.

Erin was the name of the tall girl with the awesome stride and speed. She had curly brown hair and she spoke deliberately and thoughtfully as she introduced herself. She said she was in the ninth grade at SHS (which was why I hadn't seen her in any of my classes) and that she was an athlete player. She also had a part-time job at an ice-cream parlor. Pretty cool.

Other players included Connie, who had a compact build and giggled a lot as she talked. She said she was fifteen, but she seemed younger, both in behavior and size. She went to Kelsey Middle School, also in Stoneybrook. Jojo was in my math class at SMS. I had never seen her play soccer, and I realized that she usually wore glasses, at least to math class. Sandy was taller than most of us and more strongly built. She told us, almost defiantly, that she also was in special ed at Kelsey Middle School. She said this with an almost reproachful look at Connie.

Annalise was a small, skinny, restless girl who spoke with a slight speech impediment. "I run fast," she told us. I wondered if it was true, or if it was something someone had told her. Soccer teams can get killed by having a slow player, once the other team figures it out and decides to play down that side of the field.

Not the best attitude, I know, but that's how I thought — at the time.

When we had finished introducing ourselves, the coach made random pairings of athletes and partners, and I was paired with Jeana, who was short and quick and a new convert to soccer. "My brother plays," she explained. "In school. He's at the university. I can't play with him anymore, so I joined this team."

"Cool," I said.

Coach Wu announced, "Basic skills drills, everybody. Pass the ball back and forth between each other. Practice trapping it ten times with each foot. Then take turns throwing it and practicing thigh traps and chest traps. Then ten headers."

Jeana made a face. "I don't like headers."

"The secret is not to let it hit the top of your head," I said. "That's what hurts."

We did the drills and I admit I watched Erin and her partner out of the corner of my eye. I realized that she was also working with a less-experienced player.

But the team had plenty of talent, and I began to have high hopes for Stoneybrook United. Especially with me and Erin on the team. I figured we could pose a serious scoring threat.

Coach Wu gradually increased the tempo and the skill levels of the drills until we were moving at top speed. She kept a sharp eye on us and didn't cut anyone any slack. But she didn't dog us, either. If we did something right, she let us know. If we didn't, she demonstrated the correct way to do it or asked one of the athletes or partners to demonstrate, then told us to do it again.

Annalise proved to be fast *and* quick, and I was ashamed of my earlier cynicism. I realized that I had been expecting less of the players with mental retardation, something that we had talked about not doing at the training session, and something that Coach Wu clearly didn't do.

By the time we took our water break, I was sweating. As we stood around the fountain at one corner of the field, Coach Wu studied us and then said to Petra, "Have you ever played goalie?"

Petra looked, well, petra-fied. "M-me?" she stammered.

The coach nodded. "You're quick and you attack the ball well. Those are two important qualities in a goalie."

"But I, well, I usually play on the field. In midfield," Petra said.

"We've got a lot of depth in midfield," said the coach. "And since we don't have anyone on the team with goalie experience, we can start fresh with beginners. You've played before so you know the rules. So has Sandy. Sandy, you're tall. That's useful in the goal, especially for the high shots. I'm going to ask you two to learn the position."

That caught Sandy by surprise. Her green

eyes widened, and she pushed her sweaty bangs back with both hands so that her red-blonde hair was standing up like a dandelion. "I can do that," said Sandy. But, like Petra, she didn't look entirely pleased.

"You'll both get some field time too," said Coach Wu, and she made another note on her clipboard. "I believe that players should be able to understand and handle lots of different positions."

I saw Petra make a face at Sandy and Sandy make one back. Then they both exchanged rueful grins. I knew how they felt. Playing goalie is the hardest position on a soccer team, in my opinion. The goalie, as you probably know, is the only player on the team who can use her hands to catch the ball. That's because she's standing in front of the goal, in a marked area called the goal box, and she is the last person on the defense. She has to stop the ball because if she doesn't catch it, it will go into the goal and the other team will score and win.

If the goalie is really good and does her job, no goals go in. Then if her team scores, her team wins. But who gets the credit for a win? Usually the forward — the player on the front line — who scores against the other team. The goalie hardly ever gets credit for great saves.

But if you lose, what do people remember? All those goals that went right past the goalie.

Plus, goalies have to be fearless and fast. They have to be able to jump high and dive headlong to catch shots on the ground, like a baseball player sliding into home plate.

Ugh.

Erin said, "The goalie for the Mexican national team also plays on the field sometimes. He's good."

Coach Wu said, "That's right." She checked her watch and said, "Okay, everybody hustle. We haven't got all day and I want to set up a scrimmage. We'll do some offense against defense."

I was immediately ready. The scrimmage at the end of practice is the best part of the session. After all, it's a practice game. As the coach explained to Petra and Sandy how she wanted them to stand in the goals and practice positioning themselves, but not to try to make any spectacular saves, I reknotted my shoelaces and jogged in place a little, just to show that I was ready to go.

Coach Wu surveyed the team, ran her finger down the list of players on her clipboard, then divided the team into offense (the front line, also known as forwards or strikers, and the offensive midfielders) versus the defense (the defensive midfielders and the back line, also called fullbacks or defensive backs).

The offensive positions, in case my description of how hard it is to play goalie didn't tip you off, are the plum positions on the team. You score the goals and if you make mistakes in the other team's defensive zone, it isn't usually so terrible. No one is going to steal the ball from you and shoot it into your own goal from there.

But the defensive jobs — help! One goof and the other team could easily convert your mistake into *their* goal. Serious pressure and not my idea of fun. And yet, there are people who like the job.

Amazing.

But not as amazing as the words that came out of the coach's mouth.

"Abby," she said.

I jumped to attention. "Yeah, Coach?"

"We're going to play a three-person defense, and I want you to play center fullback."

I froze. "Fullback?" I croaked.

"Yes. You're familiar with the position?"

"Sure, but I've never played it before." Clearly the coach had made a mistake. I hastened to set her right. "I'm a forward. A striker. In fact, on Long Island, where I'm from, I was the leading scorer on my team."

Coach Wu was unmoved. "I've often found that a good striker can be made, with hard work, into a good defender. After all, you have an instinct for what the offense is going to do.

With your offensive experience, you can antici-
pate and block the play."

I couldn't believe it. I opened my mouth and
then closed it again. The coach isn't always
right. But she is always the coach. I couldn't argue with her. At least not now.

But what I *could* do was show her what a
good player I was, and what a waste of scoring
opportunities it would be to keep me back on
defense. I set my jaw and forced myself not to
speak as the coach set up the scrimmage teams.

I also vowed, as we trotted out onto the field
into our positions, to stop one player FIRST.

Erin.

Because Coach Wu had given Erin my job.
My position. Erin was the center forward.

But not for long, I vowed. Not if I had anything to do with it.

# CHAPTER 4

Grand Central Station in New York City is big, beautiful, and FULL of people, all of them moving at top speed. Actually, all of New York City is like that, although not everyone would agree that it's beautiful.

But I like the feeling of swift, constant motion. I move at a pretty fast clip myself, and the New York pace makes me feel right at home.

"Abby!" cried Anna as we came up from the train platform and I paused to stare. "Don't stop now!"

"Right," I said. I took a deep breath and caught hold of the sleeve of Anna's jacket so we wouldn't be separated.

At that moment I heard a voice calling, "Anna, Abby, over here!"

"James!" Anna said and waved.

James is Mom's assistant (Mom is an executive editor at this big publishing house).

"I cut a deal with your mom — I meet your

train, put you into a cab to her office, and I leave early." James grinned and I couldn't help but grin back. He's got that kind of a smile. He's been Mom's assistant for a few years now. He's a tall, skinny guy with the longest eyelashes I've ever seen.

"This way," said James, and he led us through the station toward the cab stand. Since James was in charge, I figured I could stare at the surroundings as much as I wanted to. I did just that, letting my mouth hang open as I peered up at the golden constellations set into the sky blue ceiling of the main part of the station and read the train schedules above the ticket booths.

I kept staring as the cab zipped through the streets, fitting itself into spaces I wouldn't have attempted to shoot a soccer ball through (or, at least, that's the way it seemed). It was almost as much fun as a ride at a carnival, and I was a little sorry when it was over. I don't think Anna was, though. She sighed as she paid the driver. I think it was a sigh of relief.

"Ready?" Mom hung up the phone as we walked into her office, shoveled a stack of manuscripts into her already overstuffed briefcase, and swept us out the door of her office. She closed it behind her and said, "Italian? Is that okay?"

"It fits into my training plans," I said lightly.

I'd decided *not* to think about the disastrous soccer practice the day before. I had plenty of time to change the coach's mind and get back my position as center forward. Or I could play wing. A wing — an outside forward — was a position I could handle too.

Although most people stop working and leave their jobs at five o'clock or five-thirty, in Mom's publishing house plenty of people were still hunched over desks or staring at computer screens or talking earnestly to other people as we left at six-thirty. We stopped to say hello to a couple of people, but fortunately not many. I was hungry.

The Italian restaurant was very elegant, with acres of white tablecloths and heavy silverware and fresh flowers on every table and not a pizza in sight. "Everyone's talking about this place," Mom remarked after the host had seated us. "So I decided to bring you two to see if it passed the test before I bring any important authors."

"Gee, thanks," said Anna.

After we'd ordered and the waiter had served us an appetizer of antipasto, Mom leaned across the table and said, "Actually, there is another reason we're here tonight."

*Uh-oh*, I thought. No such thing as a free lunch. Or a free dinner.

Anna put down her fork and eyed Mom.

"Well, so far it passes the food test, in case you're interested," she said.

Were we going to move again? Or maybe it was just simple good news, like Mom had gotten a promotion at work.

But would she look so serious if it was good news?

Mom took a sip of water. She put her glass down. She picked it up again and took another sip.

A waiter appeared out of nowhere and filled her glass.

"It passes the service test so far too," I said, trying to keep things light.

But Mom didn't smile. She said, "As you know, we haven't been to the cemetery where your father is buried since we moved to Stoneybrook."

Anna and I didn't look at each other and we didn't speak.

"Your father's birthday is this month," Mom went on after a few moments. "And it's been four years since your father . . . died."

A shock went through me at the word. I stared down at my plate, my appetite deserting me.

"Okay," said Anna neutrally.

Encouraged, Mom said, "What I was thinking is that we should go visit Grandfather David and Grandmother Ruth."

David and Ruth Stevenson are my father's

parents, our paternal grandparents. We're not very close to them, even though they lived near us on Long Island. We're closer to Gram Elsie and Grandpa Morris, Mom's mother and father.

"Have they invited us?" I asked, more to say something than because I really wanted to know.

"Not exactly. But we've discussed it. I know they'd really like to see us, particularly you two."

This was not my idea of a good time. In fact, the conversation was making me very uncomfortable.

To my relief, the waiter materialized. "Is everything all right?" he asked.

"No," I wanted to say. "NO!"

But we all nodded.

"The antipasto is . . ." he paused and gestured, and we looked at the mostly uneaten plate of food.

"Very good," Mom said. She picked up a fork and stabbed a stuffed clam and held it up. "We're just taking our time enjoying it."

Satisfied, the waiter nodded and glided away. Mom ate the clam absently, then put the fork down.

Anna said slowly, "When would we go?"

*Never*, I thought.

"The weekend of your father's birthday,"

Mom said. "We could spend the night, visit his grave as a family. I know it isn't the easiest way to spend a weekend, but I think we need to do this. Family is important, and while you don't know this now, it grows more important as you get older."

Anna nodded. "Okay," she said.

I didn't say anything, which of course didn't let me off the hook. "Abby?" Mom asked.

I looked up from my intensive study of sautéed artichoke heart on my plate and said, "Well, I don't know."

Mom reached over and patted my hand. "It won't be so hard, trust me."

What could I say? I nodded, which didn't mean I agreed to go. I only nodded to show that, yes, I trusted Mom.

She didn't recognize the fine distinction, though. She patted my hand once more, then withdrew it.

Then she surveyed the antipasto as if it had just arrived at our table. "My," she said brightly, as if nothing at all were wrong. "Doesn't this look good?"

I shoveled some more food onto my plate and moved it around, eating enough so that Anna and Mom wouldn't notice or think I was sulking.

But my appetite for dinner, New York, and

just about everything else in the world was gone.

Dad was dead. Gone. He would never come back. And although I could remember him now without crying, could laugh without feeling guilty, I didn't want to go back to Long Island, didn't want to visit Grandfather David and Grandmother Ruth, who always talked about him and then kept finding similarities between him and Anna and me.

We had made a new life and we were doing fine.

Why couldn't Mom leave well enough alone?

# CHAPTER 5

Tuesday

    I have had yet another Great Idea.
I am not bragging. After all, as
Abby says, if it's the truth, what's
wrong with telling it? Besides,
this is an idea that Abby would
approve of. It all started with
a bath.

Kristy wasn't coaching the Krushers when she had her Great Idea. She was washing a car while she was baby-sitting for several Krusher team members, along with Claudia.

Car washing is not necessarily part of baby-sitting. But a good baby-sitter is prepared for anything. So when Kristy headed across the street with her stepsister, Karen (age seven); her stepbrother, Andrew (age four); and her younger brother, David Michael (age seven); she didn't freak out when she was met at the door by Linny and Hannie Papadakis (ages nine and seven), wearing raincoats, rain hats, and carrying buckets. (Her baby sister Emily Michelle was with Kristy's grandmother.)

Claudia, holding Sari Papadakis, who is two, appeared in the doorway behind them.

"It's not raining inside, is it?" asked Kristy, holding out her hand and pretending to be worried about the weather.

Hannie burst out laughing and Linny said, "Of course not."

"That's good," said Kristy, leading her crew inside, "because it makes an awful mess." She glanced at Karen. "Do you think I should carry an umbrella, just in case?"

Karen's blue eyes narrowed thoughtfully behind her glasses. Then she said, "If it rained indoors long enough, it might flood and wash all the furniture outdoors."

Hannie said, "And then it could dry and we could bring it back inside."

"But only if it stopped raining inside," said Karen.

Everyone started laughing then. When they stopped, Claudia said, "Well, it won't rain inside today, but I predict *very* local showers outside. Like in the driveway, over the Papadakises' station wagon."

"Ah," said Kristy, the light dawning.

"We're going to wash Daddy's car," said Hannie. "It needs it. It's a surprise."

"It's also good practice for when you get a car of your own," said Karen.

Linny, Karen, Andrew, and David Michael all nodded solemnly, making it very difficult for Kristy and Claudia not to laugh. Which they didn't do, although Claudia had to bury her face in Sari's soft, baby-sweet-smelling curls for a moment to hide the smile she couldn't keep off her face.

Then Claudia said, "Let me get Sari's bathing suit before we go outside."

"We need car-wash clothes too," announced Karen. (In case you haven't noticed, Karen is a stickler for detail, in addition to being very imaginative.)

"We've got lots and lots of stuff," said Hannie. "And there's more stuff in the hall closet."

In no time at all, the car-wash crew had swathed itself in rain hats, caps, and even rain boots. Then Claudia and Kristy found some buckets and sponges and everyone went outside to wash the car.

It was when they were swabbing on the soap that Kristy had her next Great Idea.

"A car wash!" she exclaimed, stopping in mid-window-wipe. "That's what we'll do."

"We're doing it already," said David Michael.

"Kristy? What is it?" asked Claudia, who was accustomed to the look that Kristy wore when she was Thinking.

"Stoneybrook United needs equipment and shirts, right?"

"Right," said Claudia.

"Well, why don't we raise some money to support them? If we all worked together, I bet we could do it."

Linny said, "What's Stoneybrook United?"

As they washed the car, Kristy and Claudia explained what the Special Olympics Unified Team was and that Abby was playing on a soccer team called Stoneybrook United.

"They don't have team shirts?" asked Karen. "You have to have shirts to be a team! It's very, *very* important."

"I know," said Kristy. "That's why I want to

raise money to help the team buy shirts."

"We could form a Booster Club," Claudia suggested, "to support Stoneybrook United."

"I want to join," said Linny instantly.

"Me too," said Karen, and all the other kids agreed.

When Kristy had calmed them down, she told them that everyone could participate.

"Let's call all the Krushers," said Karen. "They should help too."

"That's a good idea," said Kristy. "I'll call the BSC members tonight and we'll start a phone tree."

"We could have a bake sale," said David Michael.

"Or at least sell refreshments to people while they wait for us to wash their cars. Where can we hold it, though?" said Kristy.

"In our driveway!" shouted Karen in her loudest outdoor voice. "We'll make signs and put them on all the corners and we can stand on the corner of our street with a big sign and a flag to show people where to come to the car wash!"

In no time at all, the plans for the SB United Booster Club had mushroomed. (SB was our way of abbreviating Stoneybrook.) Before the Papadakises' car was clean (and it got a really good wash, because all of the kids kept scrubbing it and sloshing water over it in their excitement), the founding members of the Booster Club had decided to recruit the Krusher cheerleaders — Vanessa Pike, Haley Braddock, and Charlotte Johanssen — to cheer SB United on. The Booster Club would also make signs for the games and even make buttons to sell at the games.

By the time the car-wash crew had trooped back inside to shed rain gear and drink lemonade, Kristy knew that another Great Idea was on its way to being realized.

What she didn't know was that I wasn't ready for anyone's Great Ideas now.

# CHAPTER 6

How many practices does it take to convince a coach that she has made a mistake?

I didn't know, and I was getting over my enthusiasm for Coach Wu. In fact, I was beginning to have serious doubts about her. She might be a great softball coach, but what did she know about soccer, really? So she'd played a little varsity at UNC. That was probably years and *years* ago.

But I am not a quitter. So even though I realized that I was all wrong in a defensive position, I did my best at practice. And I kept in mind that in soccer, anyone can score. There have been great defensive players throughout the history of soccer who have done just that. When everybody on the team plays together like a team, any player can run through and use the element of surprise to take a shot on the goal. On the best teams, all the players can play all positions and switch off. Total soccer it's called.

I decided to put the total-soccer concept into effect during our scrimmage at the end of the practice. In the meantime, I concentrated on doing everything perfectly for Coach Wu. This was my last chance before our first game to convince the coach to give me the position I deserved.

Only, Erin got lucky. I mean, so she executed a few neat foot moves, did a nice give and go, and passed me to score during the scrimmage. We had a green goalie, and I'm not used to playing defense anyway.

"Concentrate, Abby," called Coach Wu. "Good work, Erin."

Erin's team cheered and they all gave each other high fives.

"Next time," I said to Erin as she walked by. I smiled to show I was joking. She smiled back and said, after a moment, "No way!"

"We'll stop 'em," said Sandy from behind me in the goal. I didn't turn around to acknowledge what she had said.

Needless to say, I stayed in center fullback position for the rest of the game. Ugh. But at least I kept Erin from scoring again.

"Good practice, guys," said Coach Wu. "Play like that in the game on Saturday and we won't have any problems."

I looked at Coach Wu in disbelief. How could we play great without me on the front line?

But everyone else was nodding enthusiastically. Then Coach Wu said, "How about some ice cream? I think we've earned it."

Jeana clapped her hands excitedly, seeming for a moment like a much younger kid. Connie, who had been playing defense with me, volunteered, "My mother has a big car. We could all ride in that."

"Not all of us," said Coach Wu, "but anyone who can't fit in Connie's mother's car is welcome to ride in my van."

I decided a ride in Coach Wu's van was just what I needed, although sharing ice cream with my teammates wasn't what I wanted at the moment.

That's how I found myself in the van with Coach Wu and half of SB United after practice.

As we drove toward the ice-cream parlor, I turned to Coach Wu and said, "Soccer is a great game, isn't it?" (I was trying to be subtle.)

"It is," she replied.

"I *love* it," cried Sandy from the backseat.

"Soccer, soccer, soccer," Petra began to chant, and the others took it up. The van was rocking. Coach Wu glanced in her rearview mirror and smiled.

"Great team spirit, isn't it?" I offered.

Coach Wu's eyes flicked toward me for an instant. I smiled. "My old team on Long Island had great team spirit too. It's why we won. Of course, you have to score to win as well. I was the leading scorer on my team. I was the center forward."

"Don't worry," said Coach Wu, and I had the feeling that she was deliberately misunderstanding me. "You'll get the hang of center back."

We pulled into the parking lot in front of 32 Flavors and Then Some.

As we piled through the front door, someone cried, "Erin! Hey, girl, what are you doing here on your day off?"

Erin grinned. "Hello, Mr. Carr. I've been playing soccer," she said.

The big man behind the counter grinned broadly. "Good. It means you'll eat more ice cream."

"I want extra-big scoops for all my friends," said Erin.

*What a show-off*, I thought. I had forgotten about her part-time job.

But no one else seemed to think so. They crowded around Erin, asking her questions, pointing to all the different flavors, and basking in the attention that Mr. Carr and the other employees were lavishing on her and "her friends."

I hung back, staying a little separate, but not too much. I hadn't forgotten that Coach Wu was lurking. I didn't want her to think I had a bad attitude or anything.

But when Erin turned to me and asked, "What kind of ice cream do you want, Abby?" I couldn't help myself. I snapped, "I can order for myself. I'm not a baby."

Erin frowned. A hurt look came into her eyes. Then anger replaced it. "Okay," she said. She turned back to the counter.

I ordered vanilla and sat at the end of the table, as far from Erin as I could get.

I was also as far from my team as I had ever been from any team of which I had been a part. On Long Island, I would have been laughing and joking with my teammates. We would have been doing all the silly things that teammates — and friends — do: pretending our straws were stupid mustaches, making loud slurping noises, ragging on each other about how we had played, talking about upcoming games.

But Stoneybrook United wasn't like that. *Everybody*, I thought sourly, *is treating Erin like a star.*

*What a show-off*, I thought again. *And what a bunch of phonies.* It was one thing to shine at practices, in no-pressure situations.

It was quite another not to crack under pressure at the games.

Erin would crack. I was sure of it.

And the team would lose.

*Ha*, I thought, and slurped my vanilla ice cream all alone.

# CHAPTER 7

"What a great day for soccer," said Sandy.

"Every day is a great day for soccer," I answered automatically. I checked the heavy silver tape that held each of my lucky cleats together in one piece. Should I add another wrap before the game, or would they hold up?

I decided they would hold up. The big shoe companies make soccer cleats for women now (and it's about time), and I had tried on several pairs, including this pair of Adidas that . . .

But no use thinking about that now. My lucky cleats had gotten me through too many games to abandon them while they had a single kick left in them. That's why I babied them along, only wearing them for games, keeping them supplied with new shoelaces and plenty of protective polish.

"I'd rather play in weather like this than in rain. Or snow," said Erin, who was sitting nearby.

"A good player can play in any weather," I said snappishly.

I had insulted Erin, and some of the players knew it. Sandy glanced at me in confusion and surprise. Petra took in a sharp breath.

Erin didn't seem to notice. She answered immediately, with annoying self-confidence, "Then I'm not worried."

A few people laughed, and I saw Sandy and Petra relax visibly.

The truth? Okay, I was a little ashamed of taking a shot at Erin. But I was angry too. She had my position, and I was stuck in the hard-work-for-no-glory, kill-or-be-killed zone of the soccer field.

I didn't think it was fair. I didn't think she'd earned it. But if we lost today, who would be blamed? Not the offense for not scoring, but the defense for letting the other team score against us.

After Coach Wu went over the lineup with us, the referee checked all our equipment to make sure it conformed to the league rules. (Shin guards are required, and you can't wear metal cleats, for example, or potentially dangerous jewelry such as earrings, which can get ripped out of your earlobe.)

Coach Wu had designated Jojo, who wasn't varsity but did an okay job at soccer in PE, and Erin (who else) as co-captains of the first game.

They shook hands with the captain of the other team. Then the referee tossed a coin to see who won the right to choose which team got the ball first and which end they got to defend.

After that, we ran out onto the field and got into our positions. I danced in place from one foot to the other and studied our opponents as I waited for the starting whistle. Was the tall, pale blonde girl on the left wing as fast as her long legs seemed to indicate? Or was she one of those tall people who trips over her own feet? Still, her height could be a problem close to the goal because clumsy or not, she could get up to head the ball in. A small dark-skinned girl with black hair in tiny braids who was in center midfield position also worried me. In my experience on the soccer field, small people are often fast and sneaky and very aggressive. I wonder if they're extra aggressive because they're short.

One girl who was in left midfield I recognized as having Down syndrome. She was wearing a layer of long underwear under her uniform. (I remembered that people with Down syndrome often caught colds more easily.) She looked strong and competent. I'd have to keep an eye on her too.

I sighed inwardly. Defense was way too much responsibility.

One thing was certain: The other team had

better uniforms — real uniforms. The Stoney-brook United team members were all wearing purple shirts with the numbers put on the back in white tape.

The whistle blew and I forgot about uniforms.

From the sidelines I heard "YEAAAAAA UNITED!" and looked over to see every member of the BSC plus what looked like at least half of our sitting charges. They were holding up signs and clapping and cheering loudly. I smiled and waved and went to work.

It would not do to let the fans down.

But I did.

I don't know what happened. I'd take the ball and try to dribble it up to get a shot, and I'd lose it. More than once, when I was on a really good roll toward the goal, I would hear Coach Wu shout, "ABBY! GET BACK IN POSITION!"

At first I did, as soon as I took the shot. But when the other team scored twice on us, I began to ignore her. Somebody had to score, and it didn't look like our front line was up to it.

Our team clearly didn't understand the concept of total soccer. When I went forward, I got no support. None of my teammates dropped back to cover for me. No one ran alongside so I could pass to her in case I needed to. The defensive players swarmed over me, and even I could not work my way out of such heavy traffic in front of the goal to get off a shot.

Erin scored one goal. A defender had stolen the ball from me, and before she could clear it out, Annalise, one of our wings, had tapped it free. It skidded to Erin's feet and she fired at the goal. Since she was only a few feet away, she could hardly have missed.

It was luck.

My bad luck.

We ended the game 2–1.

I was in no mood for the pep talk Coach Wu made after the game, and I tuned her out as she rambled on and on about position and teamwork.

I didn't want to smile when Karen led the charge of BSC members and kids, crying, "We're the Stoneybrook United Booster Club. See?" She pointed to a button on her jacket that read, STONEYBROOK UNITED *RULES*.

"Nice button," I said, forcing myself to smile. "You guys were really cheering too." I could hear the lack of joy in my voice, but fortunately Karen and the other kids didn't. Karen beamed.

Charlotte Johanssen said, "We'll have better cheers next time. Then you'll win."

"It's not your fault we lost, Char. You guys were great." Anger at the memory of how we had lost the game added new warmth to my voice. "Really great," I added. "Thanks."

"Next game," said Kristy.

"Yeah," I said. I walked away, in Erin's direction. If Coach Wu wasn't going to do anything, maybe Erin and I could have a little talk and straighten out her problems.

Erin looked up and smiled at me as she dragged her cleats off and stuffed them into her gear bag. "We'll win next time," she said cheerfully.

"Good game," I forced myself to say with a phony smile.

"Thank you," said Erin, almost formally.

I waited, but she didn't tell me I had played a good game. Not that it mattered.

"I think our team could be a winning team," I went on. Erin stood up and hoisted her gear bag to her shoulder. She didn't say anything, but she looked at me intently. "But we have to play like a team," I said. "For example, I could have scored several times today if the rest of the team had given me the support I needed."

Erin frowned as she was turning my words over and over in her head. Then she said, "But you play defense. They scored because you weren't in your place."

My mouth dropped open. "What?"

"You didn't stay where you were supposed to stay," she said.

"I ran through with the ball," I said. "It's

called total soccer, and someone on our team was supposed to cover for me."

Erin shook her head. "Coach Wu said for you to stay in your place and you didn't."

"Excuse me," I said with elaborate courtesy, "but I think I know a little bit more about soccer than you do."

That's when Erin got me. "Why?" She looked at me directly, and I saw a flash of anger in her eyes. "Because I have mental retardation? Do you think I can't play as well as you because of that?"

"I didn't say that!" I cried.

"I stay in my position. And I scored. *I am* a good player. Better than you," she said.

I couldn't believe my ears. "That's what you think," was the best I could manage before I turned and stalked away.

As I did, I heard the Boosters launch into a huge cheer for Stoneybrook United. I looked up to see the rest of the team converging on its new Booster Club, and I made myself scarce.

"How did you do?" asked Anna as I trudged past her room to my own. She was practicing her violin.

"If you'd been there, you'd know," I said, even though I hadn't expected Anna or Mom to show up. In fact, I'd told them to come later in the season when the team was "more together." Translation: By then, I figured I'd have my spot as center forward.

"You lost," guessed Anna.

"Yeah. So?" I snapped. I stomped to my room, fell across the bed sideways, and flung one arm over my eyes.

"Abby?"

"Hi, Mom," I said, without removing my arm.

"You okay?"

"Fine," I said wearily.

She came into my room and I felt the bed sink as she sat down on one side of it. "I'm guessing you lost today."

"Yeah."

"It's just the first game. There will be others."

"I know."

After a moment, Mom said, "So about our trip to Long Island."

"What about it?"

"Abby, I don't like your tone of voice."

"And I don't like the idea of going to Long Island. It's not like I was asked if I wanted to go. You tried to trick us into agreeing by taking us to some fancy New York restaurant."

"Abby!"

"Well, it won't work. I don't want to go. I think it is a bad idea. A very bad idea. Rotten, in fact." I sat up and glared at my mother as if she were an enemy soccer player in my territory. "You can't bribe me with dinner like I'm one of your stupid authors or something."

That did it. With two spots of color burning on her cheeks, my mother stood up. She said, "I think we've discussed this enough. We'll talk about it more when you are less upset about losing a soccer game."

"I'm not upset," I practically shouted. "Why don't you just leave me alone!"

"Certainly." Mom walked across the room and out the door, closing it firmly behind her.

I flopped back down and threw my arm across my eyes. I felt the hot sting of tears against my eyelids, but of course I wasn't going to cry.

The words of an old song came back to me.

*Alone again.*

*Naturally.*

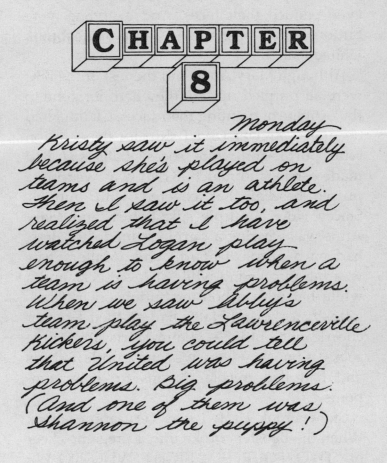

# CHAPTER 8

Monday

Kristy saw it immediately because she's played on teams and is an athlete. Then I saw it too, and realized that I have watched Logan play enough to know when a team is having problems. When we saw Abby's team play the Lawrenceville Kickers, you could tell that United was having problems. Big problems. (And one of them was Shannon the puppy!)

The Booster Club arrived in fine form. Everyone was wearing the Stoneybrook United colors of purple and white. Some of the kids had even painted their faces. And everyone wore buttons with slogans like, "I'm a Stoneybrook United Fan."

Although Mary Anne and the rest of the BSC were all purpled up too, they had not gone to the extreme of painting their faces. Claudia had decorated an oversized T-shirt for the occasion with purple-and-white soccer balls *and* had made earrings to match. Kristy was wearing a purple baseball hat covered with buttons. Stacey wore a purple silk T-shirt, and Mary Anne was wearing a purple striped shirt. Jessi had on a purple leotard, while Mallory was wearing purple-and-white-striped socks and a white hat with a booster button on it. Charlotte, Vanessa, and Haley had on their Krusher cheerleader outfits — denim skirts and white socks — but they were wearing purple T-shirts and had tied purple ribbons to their pompoms.

Stoneybrook United was very appreciative. When the Boosters broke into a pregame cheer of "TWO, FOUR, SIX, EIGHT, WHO DO WE APPRECIATE?" the team members put their heads together, then came up with a cheer of their own: "LOOK IN THE STANDS! HOORAY FOR OUR FANS!"

Silly but nice.

It didn't take Mary Anne long to notice that I wasn't smiling. In fact, I was scowling.

"Wow," Mary Anne said softly to Kristy. "Abby really does take sports seriously."

Kristy glanced over toward me and said, "I guess so. We should have known, though."

On the other side of Kristy, Claudia laughed. "We've never seen her play, but it shouldn't surprise us."

Still, it seemed extreme to Mary Anne that I not only did not say hello to them, but I never once looked in their direction. Nor did I say much of anything to any of my teammates, even when the team was warming up.

Mary Anne knew some of the students from Stoneybrook Middle School, of course. Others she didn't recognize. But as she watched them warm up, she soon realized both teams had players who had a wide range of skill levels. Some were clearly beginners. Some were not very good. Others were obviously more skilled, more experienced. Some of the players acted a little young for their ages, giggling and squealing as they kicked the ball or ran up and down the field warming up.

But overall, Mary Anne couldn't really tell

who were the partners and who were the athletes. Both were teams, she realized, much like any other team.

Except that before the first half was over, it was all too clear that my team was having problems.

And that I was definitely one of those problems.

"What's Abby doing?" asked Stacey. "She keeps running up the field with the ball and then losing it."

"She's not passing it," said Kristy grimly.

Logan, who had just arrived, said, "What position is she playing?"

"I don't know," Mary Anne said.

Suddenly, Erin burst through the pack of players with the ball at her feet. She faked left and dodged right around a defender, pulled her foot back, and launched a rocket shot into the high right corner of the goal.

The goalie never had a chance.

The Stoneybrook United players who were on the bench erupted into cheers. "GO, ERIN!" they shouted.

The three booster cheerleaders picked up on Erin's name and began, "TWO, FOUR, SIX, EIGHT, WHO DO WE APPRECIATE? ERIN ERIN *ERIN!*"

Out on the field, Erin's teammates converged on her, slapping her on the back and leaping and skipping with joy. Even the goalie ran out from the goal to give Erin a celebratory thump on the shoulder.

But I didn't.

Mary Anne watched in amazement as I coolly trotted back into my position without even a show of excitement that the team was now ahead, 1–0.

But the Booster Club didn't notice.

"This is *great*," Mary Anne heard Karen say in her loudest outdoor voice to Hannie Papadakis. "I'm going to be a soccer player someday and have everybody cheer for me!"

"Me too," said Hannie instantly.

Behind the two girls, Shannon the puppy began to bark excitedly as David Michael and Linny Papadakis raced up and down the sidelines, shouting encouragement.

Mary Anne, Kristy, and Claudia looked over at them, smiling at their enthusiasm. Then, suddenly, Shannon veered to one side, pulling David Michael with her. She pulled him into the middle of some of the Kickers, who were doing a passing drill with an extra ball on the sidelines.

"Look," said Hannie. "Shannon's playing soccer."

"Woof, woof," barked Shannon excitedly, charging for the ball.

"No, Shannon. Stop! Stay! Come!" gasped

David Michael. At that moment he tripped and fell and lost his grip on the leash.

Shannon butted the ball with her head and it rolled away from her. She wagged her tail even faster as she decided that she had invented a new game. She chased the ball and crashed into it again as the Kickers began to laugh and run after her.

As neatly as if she had been playing soccer all her life, Shannon dodged the players, still keeping the ball.

"Oh, no!" said Kristy. She could see what was going to happen next. She took off after Shannon, along with the Lawrenceville players and David Michael and Linny.

"Shannon, come back!" David Michael cried.

Shannon ignored him. She pushed the ball ahead of her with her nose — straight toward the field.

The referee blew his whistle and the game began again. One of the Kickers sent a long pass downfield. Her left wing ran after it, never taking her eyes from the ball.

She didn't even see Shannon.

"NOOOO!" shouted Kristy — and half a dozen other fans and players.

But it was no use. The Kicker wing tripped over Shannon and went flying through the air. Shannon spun around with a yelp of surprise.

Jojo jumped on the end of Shannon's leash

with both feet and brought her to a stop as the referee began to blow his whistle again.

Shannon began to lick the ear of the Kicker who was still sprawled on the ground.

"I'm sorry," David Michael panted, his face very red.

The wing sat up. Shannon licked her chin and the girl began to laugh. "Wow," she said. "That was an amazing tackle."

"You're not hurt?" asked Kristy.

"No," said the girl. "Just surprised."

The referee ran to them. "Which team is this dog registered to play on?" he asked.

David Michael looked anxious. "She's not on a team, but she's an SB United Booster Club member."

"If she's not registered, she can't play," said the referee, his face serious but his eyes crinkling at the corners with suppressed laughter. "She'll have to leave the field."

"Y-yes, sir!" said David Michael. "Come on, Shannon!" He took the leash from Kristy and ran off the field.

"Sorry about that," said Kristy.

"No problem," said the referee. He picked up the ball. "Drop ball from where the play stopped," he decreed.

He waited until everyone but the people who were supposed to be on the field had left. Then the wing and Jojo faced off as the referee dropped the ball and both tried to kick it. The Kicker wing got it and Jojo took off after her.

"That was awesome," said Karen. "Maybe I'll be a dog trainer and train a dog soccer team."

Kristy's eyes met Mary Anne's and she, Mary Anne, and Claudia all burst out laughing.

At halftime, the Booster Club did a brisk business in button sales. Karen attached buttons to Shannon's collar, and she and David Michael walked the puppy through the crowd. "Buy your official SB United button from the team mascot!" Karen called.

The three cheerleaders did button cheers: "Don't just shout, don't just scream! Buy a button and help your team!"

Over by the SB United bench, we drank water and Gatorade and listened intently as Coach Wu talked and drew diagrams on her clipboard.

"It's a good game," Jessi said.

"I hope our team wins," Mallory added.

Kristy looked thoughtful, but she didn't say anything. Logan said, "They could use some practice on their teamwork. They're not moving the ball around very well. You can't rely on just one player to score for you."

Mary Anne remained silent too, watching the SB United team as Coach Wu talked. She saw me look up suddenly and speak. The coach said something and I said something back. The coach shook her head. I flung one arm out and pointed toward Erin. Erin immediately pointed back and we glared at each other.

We reminded Mary Anne of two little kids about to have a fight on the playground.

Coach Wu said something that stopped the fight. I looked down again and Erin tilted her chin up and looked away. Coach Wu looked from me to Erin, then began drawing another diagram on her clipboard.

I didn't start the second half. Many players didn't, but Erin did.

As the game went on, I sat stiffly on the bench, my arms folded.

Then Mary Anne watched a heavyset girl who didn't run much but always seemed to be in the right place at the right time jump up as a high ball was crossed in front of the goal. She hit the ball with a twist of her body and headed it in for the Kickers.

A groan went up from the SB United fans, while the Kickers fans went wild.

The score was now 1–1.

"Oh, no!" shouted Haley. "The Lawrenceville footballers are ahead!"

Karen frowned. "They're playing soccer," she said.

"Whatever," said Haley.

Karen put her hands on her hips. She is a stickler for rules, and it was easy to see that she felt as if someone weren't sticking to the rules. But before she could argue, Vanessa said, "We've got to get another goal before the Kickers get on a roll." Even in times of crisis, Vanessa usually doesn't forget she wants to be a poet.

"Get that goal back, GETTHATGOAL-BACK!" Charlotte began to shout. The other cheerleaders took up the cheer and soon the fans were rocking the sidelines.

Shannon barked and pulled on her leash and managed to move David Michael a few feet toward the field. Then Linny caught hold of the leash too, and both boys held on and kept Shannon from racing out on the field to try and even the score.

I had leaped to my feet, my fists clenched. I heard the fans, but barely. I turned blazing eyes toward Coach Wu, and as if she could feel the heat of my stare, Coach Wu looked over her shoulder and motioned me forward. She put her hand on my shoulder and spoke into my ear about what she wanted me to do when I went back into the game.

Dancing up and down with impatience, I barely heard her. I tore out onto the field the moment the referee signaled it was okay for a substitution.

For the next few minutes, it seemed as if I were everywhere. I played furiously, madly, and because I was so fast and so aggressive, the other team was momentarily disconcerted.

"Will they do a shoot-out if they tie?" asked Mallory. "That's what they do in the triplets' league."

"I don't know," said Kristy.

As it turned out, they weren't going to find out.

The game was almost over when I took the ball away from the Lawrenceville Kicker center forward in our defensive end. I dribbled it slowly forward, almost as if I were daring the other team to come and get me.

"Shouldn't she pass it?" Mary Anne asked Logan.

"Score, score, score some more!" the cheerleaders chanted.

"Kick it in, let's win!" Vanessa added.

"U-NI-TED, U-NI-TED!" Mallory and Jessi began to scream, jumping up and down.

"Not necessarily. That's a good strategy. She's drawing the opposition's players toward her. When they move toward her, they create open space for the United players to move into," Logan answered Mary Anne.

I kept going.

"Now," muttered Logan.

"Pass it," Kristy said through gritted teeth at the same moment.

But I pulled the ball back with the sole of my foot, stepped over it, and rolled around the defender.

"Wow!" shouted Linny. "Cool move."

From the side of the field, Erin raised her hand and waved it.

"That means pass it to her, right?" asked Hannie. She and Karen had come to stand by Kristy, Claudia, Mary Anne, and Logan.

"Isn't she supposed to pass it now?" asked Karen. Even she could see that I wasn't playing like a team member, that I was hogging the ball when I should be passing.

Suddenly Erin darted across the front of the goal.

"Kick it to Erin!" shouted Karen.

Although I didn't hear Karen, I looked up. Erin — if she had the ball — would have an excellent shot on the goal. She could score the winning goal and be a hero.

I pulled my foot back — and took the shot myself.

"Oh, *no*," cried Karen, clutching Hannie's arm with both hands.

"Uh-oh," said Hannie, softly. The ball hit one

of the SB United midfielders and rebounded out. Erin darted forward and got it.

The cheerleaders froze. Kristy saw that Charlotte had her hands over her ears, her eyes wide. Vanessa had her hands over her mouth. And Haley had her eyes shut tight.

I ran toward an open spot. Now I had a clear shot at the goal. "Erin!" I screamed. "Over here!"

Everyone on the sidelines, and on SB United, seemed to freeze as Erin did exactly what I had just done. She took the shot herself.

It rebounded again and a Kicker midfielder swooped down on it and raced toward midfield.

"NO, NO, NO!" screamed Karen.

"GO, GO, GO," screamed Vanessa. "Go *get* her!"

It took only three neat passes and the Kicker forward ran right through the hole in the middle of the defense, where I should have been, and kicked the ball into the goal.

The referee blew his whistle. The game was over.

"The Kickers kicked us and licked us," said Vanessa sadly.

Haley opened her eyes. "Is it over?"

"Yes," said Charlotte. "We lost."

Shannon stopped barking, almost as if she understood, and sat down.

As the Kickers players and fans swarmed the field cheering madly, I stalked toward Erin.

Erin met me halfway. From the sidelines, Coach Wu saw what was happening and started toward both of us.

"This isn't good," said Kristy.

Coach Wu didn't reach Erin and me soon enough.

"What were you *doing*?" I shouted. "I was open. I could have made the winning goal!"

"I was open too," Erin shouted back. "You should have passed it to me!"

"And watch you blow the shot? What are you, stupid?" I shouted back, loudly enough for the whole world to hear.

On the sidelines, Karen frowned ferociously. "You're not ever supposed to call anybody stupid," she said.

No one answered. No one spoke for what seemed an eternity.

Then Erin leaped toward me with her fists clenched. I raised my own fists, ready to swing back.

Coach Wu caught me by the arm and Erin by the wrist in an iron grip. Erin pulled in vain, as if more than anything in the world, she wanted to pound on me. I yanked in her direction, my other fist clenched too.

"They're not going to fight, are they?" asked David Michael in shock.

"No, of course not," said Mary Anne with a conviction she didn't feel.

Erin stopped struggling. I lowered my clenched fist. We stared at each other wordlessly. Then Erin said in a low voice, "I'm not stupid. You're stupid. A big stupid showoff. You're the one who lost the game."

Coach Wu said, "That's enough, both of you! Go to the bench and wait for me there!"

Without looking at each other, Erin and I walked off the field and took seats at opposite ends of the bench from each other.

We were still sitting there as the Booster Club, the rest of the fans, and the two teams left. Mary Anne looked back over her shoulder and saw Coach Wu motion to the two of us to sit together at the center of the bench. She saw the coach put her hands on her hips.

"They're in trouble, aren't they?" asked Hannie.

"Because they were bad sports, right?" added Linny.

"Yes," said Mary Anne, and this time the conviction in her voice was heartfelt. "They're in trouble. Big trouble."

Karen said, "When I'm a famous soccer player, I'm never going to act like that and be a bad sport."

"Me either," said Hannie.

"Nope," agreed Linny and David Michael,

and the rest of the Booster Club took up the chorus.

Mary Anne nodded. "I hope not," she said and thought to herself that at least the Booster Club had learned something from the bad example Erin and I had set.

She just hoped we would come to our senses too, before it was too late.

# CHAPTER 9

Benched. For two whole games. In my entire soccer life, nothing like this had ever happened to me.

And all because of Erin.

I was mortified. I sat there as Coach Wu's words poured over me, my mind catching on the word "benched."

"Abby! Are you listening to me?" she asked. Her voice was soft but very serious.

"You can't bench me," cried Erin. "It's not fair."

For once we agreed on something. It wasn't fair. I was even willing to admit that Erin didn't deserve it either.

But Erin's next words put a lid on my empathy. "Abby started it."

It was such a little-kid thing to say that I looked over at Erin in surprise. She was sitting bolt upright on the bench, her hands clenched into two fists, her gaze fastened on Coach Wu's face. She looked as if she were about to cry.

Coach Wu said, "You are both responsible for your behavior today, which was one of the worst examples of unsporting conduct I have ever seen, especially between two teammates."

"I would've scored," I protested, "if Erin — "

Holding up her hand, Coach Wu stopped me. "That's not the point. And neither you, Abby, nor you, Erin, is getting the point. Your behavior is not in keeping with the spirit of the Special Olympics. It is not in keeping with the spirit of Unified Sports. It is not in keeping with the spirit of *any* athletic endeavor. Benching is a drastic measure and no coach, especially in Unified Sports, ever wants to do something like this. But I'm going to. What I saw today was players playing selfishly, behaving badly, and letting their team down."

That stopped me. Then I thought, *It can't be true.*

Coach Wu said, "I expect you to be at practice and at the next two games. I expect you to think about what you've done. And if I believe that you have made some changes in your attitudes, we'll see if you can play like members of a team after that."

"But Coach!" Erin said.

Coach Wu shook her head, turned, and walked away.

Erin jumped up and picked up her gear bag.

76

She turned to me with blazing eyes. "You are a big jerk, Abby," she said, and, still wearing her cleats, she turned and left me sitting there, speechless.

I didn't tell anybody I'd been benched. It was too humiliating. I figured I'd just go to the games and sit on the bench and people would think the coach wasn't playing me. Maybe I'd mention that she didn't like me. Or refer casually to the slightly sprained ankle I'd gotten in practice.

It was a lie about the ankle, but it was better than the truth.

Fortunately, I didn't mention a bogus bad ankle to Anna or Mom when I told them I'd lost the game.

Anna took the news lightly. "Hey," she said, "how do you get to Carnegie Hall? Practice!"

It's a dumb old joke, but one that we usually laugh at. I didn't laugh. I said, "Carnegie Hall doesn't rank with me, Anna, thanks all the same."

Anna's brows drew together in a frown. "You know what, Abby? You're turning into a real crank. Maybe this Unified Team soccer isn't right for you."

"Why don't you just go to . . . to . . . to Carnegie Hall," I retorted and left her standing in the kitchen, looking bewildered and angry.

After that I kind of shut down. I stopped listening whenever Mom and Anna discussed the plans for the trip to Long Island to visit our grandparents. It was only when my mother said at the dinner table on Thursday night that she was leaving work early on Friday so that we could get a head start on our trip to Long Island that I roused myself from my soccer stupor.

"What?" I said.

"I'm going to pick you up tomorrow afternoon," Mom repeated. "So pack your suitcases and be ready by tomorrow afternoon when I get home from the office."

"Is Grandmother making Shabbat dinner on Friday night?" asked Anna.

Mom nodded. "And we're going to synagogue. We'll go to visit your father's grave early on Sunday morning before we head back to Stoneybrook."

"I can't go," I blurted out.

"What?" Mom looked shocked. "What did you say?"

"I can't go."

"Abby, what are you talking about? I know you've been reluctant to do this, but believe me . . ."

"It's not that," I said. "I do want to see Grandmother Ruth and Grandfather David. But we've got a very important game on Saturday and I can't miss it."

"You can't miss *one* game, Abby?" Anna asked.

"It's not just any game," I said. "If we lose this one, we're out of the running for the tournament."

"The team doesn't depend on *you*, you know," argued Anna.

"I made a commitment," I said. "If I don't show up, I'm letting the team down. And it's just as important for me to show up for this game as it is for you to show up for a recital. I'm part of the team the same way you're part of the orchestra." (Coach Wu would have been surprised to hear that.)

Mom was looking thoughtful — and a little sad. "You're right, Abby, you did make a commitment, and it is an important one." She sighed.

Guilt washed over me, but I pushed it away.

Mom sighed again and got up. "Let me call Kristy's mom. You can stay at Kristy's."

"Okay," I said.

And that is how on Friday, I went to Kristy's house after the BSC meeting while my mother and my sister left for Long Island.

# CHAPTER 10

"You need a ride to your game this morning?" Mr. Brewer asked me at breakfast.

Breakfast at Kristy's house is very different from breakfast at my house. In my family, whoever gets up first makes coffee. Then each of us fixes whatever she wants. Anna and I usually get up long before our mother does, and I suspect it is the smell of the coffee that eventually drags Mom out of sleep and into the day.

At Kristy's house, it was as if several meals were being prepared and cooked at once. Nannie was making oatmeal for herself, Emily Michelle, and David Michael. Kristy was putting peanut butter on a toasted bagel for herself. I had opted for a plain bagel, which was also toasting. Meanwhile, Mrs. Brewer was drinking hot tea and eating a piece of toast. Mr. Brewer had made himself an egg sandwich out of Eggbeaters (which are sort of fake eggs that don't have any cholesterol in them — he has to be careful about that because he had a mild heart attack not too long ago) and drinking decaffeinated coffee. Charlie was drinking coffee loaded with sugar and cream and dunking his bagel into it. He'd already polished off some oatmeal. Sam was poking sleepily at a waffle topped with syrup and butter and drinking chocolate milk.

Normally I would have been fascinated by this foray into a family's morning culinary habits. But I was too glum to do more than nibble my bagel and mull over having to go to a soccer game in which I wasn't going to be allowed to play.

I'd kept a low profile at practice over the past week, hoping that might make Coach Wu relent. But the coach is the relentless type, and no matter how careful I was to stay in position and do just what she wanted, she showed no signs of calling off the two-game bench decree. Erin and I avoided each other. Most of the other kids on the team seemed to be avoiding us too. Or, at least, they didn't seem very comfortable around us.

"Abby?" Kristy waved her half-eaten bagel in front of my face. "You in there?"

"Don't play with your food, Kristy," Charlie said, and laughed as if he'd said something funny.

With a start, I came back to the present.

"What? A ride? No," I said. "No, thank you. I'm going to ride my bike. It helps me, uh, get warmed up," I babbled. "In fact, I'd better get going." Putting down my half-eaten bagel, I leaped to my feet to make my escape.

"See you at the game," Kristy said.

That stopped me. "At the game?" Did my voice sound shrill and guilty to Kristy or did it seem that way only to my own ears? "Oh, you don't need to do that. It's not that big a deal. I mean, the Sheridan Stars are not that great a team. Save it for a really good game." Like two games from now, I added silently.

"You said that at our meeting yesterday," Kristy reminded me. "And we told you that true fans go to *every* game."

"Yeah, well." Actually, everyone at the BSC meetings had been amazingly tactful, not asking me one single question about the blowup they had witnessed at the game against the Kickers. They'd talked enthusiastically of what fun it was to be a booster and made plans for the car wash to be held on Sunday afternoon.

And they hadn't taken any of my hints to just forget about Stoneybrook United, at least for now.

Kristy said in what was for her a comforting tone, "You know, losing isn't that big a deal. We still like cheering the team on."

Losing was not the problem here. Just being on the team was. But it was too late to start telling the truth. I gave up, hoisted my pack over my shoulders, and said, "See ya."

It was not a great start to what became an increasingly rotten day. In fact, the day could have taken the title from one of the picture books that is a favorite among our charges: *Alexander and the Terrible, Horrible, No Good, Very Bad Day*. Substitute *Abby* for *Alexander* and you get the picture.

I warmed up with the team. Jeana, Jojo, Annalise, and most of the other kids were sympathetic (although Petra avoided Erin and me like the plague, almost as if she were afraid she might get benched by association). As I jogged and stretched and practiced passing drills and heading drills, I tried to ignore the sea of purple flooding the bleachers. But when the familiar "TWO, FOUR, SIX, EIGHT," cheer began, I could ignore our fans no longer. I forced myself to turn and smile and wave.

Half a dozen kids happily waved back and called my name. "Your friends are nice," said Sandy. "It's great that they come to the game and cheer for you."

"They're cheering for us all," I said. "The whole team. You can't cheer for just one player."

Sandy nodded seriously. Then she grinned. "I hope they cheer for me, though. I hope I score a goal and they cheer for me!"

"Yeah, I like that part too," I said.

"I don't know. I haven't scored a goal. Not yet," said Sandy. She sighed. "And now I play goalie."

"Not all the time. You'll get a chance to score," I predicted. "Just keep practicing. I practice soccer every single day, even when it isn't soccer season."

"I know," said Sandy. "I try to too. Now I'll be glad if I don't let the other team score on me!" The referee called us together and went through the uniform and cleat check. I felt like asking why I even had to bother, but I knew better. Coach Wu might have benched me permanently.

The game started and I joined Erin and some of the others who weren't starting players on the bench. For practically the first time since I began playing soccer, I wasn't a starting player.

The Stars were a good team, but our front line was faster than their defense. It wasn't long before Annalise sent a short chip forward over the fullback's head. Jojo followed it and basically ran it into the goal, falling over the goalie in the process.

The crowd rose to its feet.

"Yellow card?" I breathed. A yellow card is a

dire warning that the referee could give to a player for any serious infraction of the rules. And most referees are very, very strict about roughing up the goalie in any way. Some of them not only give out yellow cards but take back goals scored when goalies get knocked down. Plus, two yellow cards is an automatic red card, which means you're out of the game *and* your team can't replace you. They have to play the rest of the game one player short.

It's fair. Goalies can get hurt since they are basically defenseless. When she is diving or jumping for a ball, a goalie is not thinking about protecting herself — she's thinking about stopping the goal.

But the goalie rolled over and got up laughing. The referee ran to her and said something. She shook her head and reached out to pat the opposing player on the shoulder.

The referee said something to Jojo, clearly warning her to be more careful. Then she blew her whistle and motioned for the ball to be returned to the midfield kickoff point to start the game again.

Behind me, the Booster Club began to chant, "ONE, TWO, THREE, FOUR, GET THAT GOAL, THEN GET SOME MORE."

But SB United didn't get another goal before halftime. In fact, the Stars goalie did a great job, even punching a shot she couldn't quite reach up and over the top of the net.

That brought me to my feet. "Good goalie!" I shouted, even though she was the goalie for the other team. You've got to appreciate good soccer playing by whoever is playing it.

I looked down the bench and saw that Erin was also on her feet, and that she was staring at me. Why did she look so surprised? I said, defensively, "It was a good play."

"I know," said Erin.

Then I remembered that I wasn't speaking to Erin and turned my head away. "Go team!" I shouted. "Keep up the good work!"

At halftime I felt a hand on my shoulder and looked back to see Kristy's stepsister, Karen. She leaned over and whispered loudly in my ear, "Don't worry. You'll get to play some next inning." She paused, then said, "No, I mean, second half."

I made myself smile. "Thanks, Karen," I said.

She said, still in an outdoor voice whisper, "Not all the Krushers play at once either. Sometimes I don't play for part of the game. Even really good people like Linny don't play all the time."

"I'll keep that in mind," I said.

"I'll tell Erin too," said Karen, and moved away before I could stop her.

Great. Everyone, even the kids, had noticed that I was sitting on the bench. And they'd also noticed that Erin was the only other full-time benchwarmer.

Then I realized that if Karen spoke to Erin, she might find out the truth. I started to get up and stop her, then realized it was too late. Karen had put her hand up to her mouth and was staring at Erin, her eyes wide behind her glasses. She looked over at me, then back at Erin. "I'm sorry," she said loudly to Erin.

I saw Erin blush and I felt my own cheeks redden. Worse, as Karen sped back toward the Booster Club and yanked on Kristy's arm, I knew that she was telling Kristy the truth. I wasn't sitting on the bench, waiting for the coach to put me in.

*Thanks a lot, Erin*, I thought.

The Booster Club still cheered, and they cheered United to victory, even without Erin and me on the field. We won 1–0. As the teams were shaking hands after the game, I thought, *If I'd been in the game, it would have been a blowout. I'd have scored at least two or three more goals.*

Duh, Abby. What difference did it make? We'd won. And maybe it was just as well we hadn't trounced the other team. After all, as the goalie for the Stars had said cheerfully to Petra, who'd been playing goalie for us second half, "This is the least we've ever lost by. We're getting better!"

As I walked off the field, I saw the Booster Club swarming around United. But no one talked to me. The word was out, and I couldn't decide if the BSC was being tactful or just showing its anger because I had lied.

Kristy's emotions were less of a mystery, however. She was watching me with her hands on her hips. When she caught my eye, she gave me a hard look. Then she turned and left the field.

# CHAPTER 11

Sunday

It had to hapen, rihgt? If you have a car wasch, your going to have allot of fun. and your also going to have at leest one big water fighte.

$S$tacey's boom box was playing an old song about working in the car wash and having the blues. At the far end of the street, Linny Papadakis, Charlotte Johanssen, and Vanessa Pike were waving signs, doing impromptu cheers, and motioning for people to come to the car wash in the Thomas/Brewers' driveway. Rows of buckets, heaps of old towels and torn-up sheets, sponges, and a very large supply of soap were lined up along one side of the driveway. The hose was in place.

The Big Slosh Car Wash was in business.

Kristy's grandmother Nannie was the first customer. She rolled her old pink car (affectionately known as the Pink Clinker in Kristy's family) out of the garage and into the driveway.

A swarm of boosters surrounded it and the BSC members realized that it was going to have to channel all that car-wash enthusiasm into an organized car-washing scheme. Claudia said, "Hey, wait, you guys. Let's have the Wet Crew and the Dry Crew."

Becca Ramsey giggled. "It sounds like a diaper commercial."

"Ick!" cried Jackie Rodowsky. Known among the members of the Baby-sitters Club (who all love him madly) as the Walking Disaster because of his ability to crash into, fall over, or otherwise collide with anything in his immediate vicinity, Jackie had somehow gotten hold of the hose and was waving it in an alarming way.

Jessi said, "Jackie, let me hold that," and she managed to grab it before Jackie squirted everybody.

Mal said, "Okay, then, the Soap Squad and the Towel Squad."

Everyone agreed that they could work with those names. After a few more alarms and diversions, the two squads had been established. Becca, Haley, David Michael, and Nicky and Claire Pike were on the Soap Squad, along with Kristy, Jessi, Shannon, and Logan, with Mal in charge of the hose. The Towel Squad, responsible for wiping the cars dry, were Hannie, Jackie, Karen, and Adam, Byron, and Jordan Pike, Mal's triplet brothers, along with Jessi, Claudia, Mary Anne, and me.

Stacey was in charge of collecting the money, assisted by Andrew Brewer and Margo Pike.

Claudia noticed that when Kristy was put on the Soap Squad, I quickly volunteered to be on the Towel Squad. I was being unusually quiet too, Claudia thought. But that wasn't so mysterious. Everyone knew that I had been benched and felt bad for me (or so I later learned).

When Claudia and the rest of the BSC members had talked about it on the way home from the game, everyone agreed that it was not good that I had not told the BSC members and the Booster Club what had happened.

"But you know she was embarrassed," Mary Anne had argued. "I don't think we should get on her case about it. I mean, it must be hard enough for her, sitting on the sidelines."

Kristy had snorted but hadn't said anything, and eventually everybody agreed not to bring it up with me.

"We'll wait until she's ready to talk about it," Jessi had concluded.

Kristy had snorted again, but remained tightlipped.

Claudia wondered what was going on with Kristy and me.

But of course, the car wash was no place to ask.

When everyone had finished soaping, rinsing, and drying Nannie's car, and Stacey had officially filed the first profits in the shoe box that she was using as a cash register, Karen said, "I have a great idea!"

Everyone stared at Karen, who had flung her arms out dramatically. Then Claudia burst out laughing. "You know, Kristy, I can tell she's your sister. She has great ideas just like you do."

Both Karen and Kristy looked pleased.

"What is the great idea?" prompted Logan.

"We could borrow Nannie's car and put it on the corner with a sign on it that says, A SATIS-FIED CUSTOMER OF THE BIG SLOSH CAR WASH!"

"Excellent idea," said Kristy. "I couldn't have done better myself."

Karen said, "Of course, Nannie has to say it's okay."

Nannie laughed and shook her head. "How could I not? This is the Pink Clinker's chance to be famous."

"I think it already *is* famous," Kristy teased her grandmother.

So while Nannie drove the car down to the corner and parked it next to Linny, Charlotte, and Vanessa, Claudia and Karen went in search of poster board and some sign-making sup-plies. They emerged from the house a short time later with a big sign in purple, pink, and black. Claudia had even drawn a picture of the Pink Clinker with a smile on the grill of the car and made the two headlights into eyes.

"Isn't it beautiful?" Karen cried.

Claudia laughed and shook her head. "Let's go put it on the car," she said.

In no time at all, the car wash was doing a tidal wave of business. The sunny afternoon undoubtedly helped. But there was no ques-tion that the impromptu cheers and the Pink

Clinker had made a big contribution. Almost everyone who drove into Kristy's driveway for a car wash mentioned the big, old pink car.

"Can you make my car pink too?" one woman asked, laughing, as she pulled her blue sedan into the driveway.

"Oh, no!" exclaimed Karen. "But we can make it clean!"

"It's a good cause," said a thin man driving an old truck, and he donated extra money.

All the while, Claudia noticed, Kristy and I kept washing and drying cars without looking at each other and without talking very much to anyone.

"Is Kristy okay?" Claud whispered to Mary Anne during a break from the stream of cars that had poured in. Mary Anne shook her head.

"I don't know," she said. "I called her last night, but she didn't say much. I think it was because Abby was there."

One more clue that the problem was between Kristy and me, thought Claudia.

By three o'clock, when the car wash was officially closing, Stacey looked very pleased as she counted the money in the box. And Claudia and the rest of the BSC members were congratulating themselves on washing so many cars and making so much money without any major disasters. But just then she heard Jackie shout, "Oh, no!"

Claudia turned as Jackie, whose foot had somehow gotten stuck in one of the buckets, stumbled backward. He crashed into Mal and grabbed her. They both fell and Mal let go of the hose as she went down.

Water sprayed everywhere, drenching Claudia and everyone else who was standing nearby.

"Water fight!" bellowed Adam. He seized his bucket of rinse water and hurled it at his brothers.

That was all it took. In no time flat, soapy water, soggy towels, and screaming kids had filled the driveway.

What did the BSC do? What any experienced baby-sitters would do. They got out of the way and stood dripping and laughing as the kids worked off energy. Then after about five minutes, they waded back in and called a halt to the water fight.

"Okay, guys," said Kristy. "Come on inside and get dried off. Then we'll make some lemonade."

A cheer went up and the water fight was abandoned. A wet and happy group (with the exception of Kristy and me) trooped into Kristy's house.

"How'd we do?" Claudia asked Stacey as she tucked the box under her arm.

Stacey looked up with a grin. She was as wet as Claudia and everybody else, but she had managed to keep the cash box dry. "Let's just say," said Stacey, "that our car wash was anything but a washout."

# CHAPTER 12

My gear bag was on Kristy's queen-sized bed, and I was folding my things into it when she walked into the room.

"Your mom and sister are home," she announced. "I just saw them pull into your driveway."

"Thanks. You didn't have to keep watch for them, though. I'm going." I'd meant it to sound like a joke, but it didn't. It sounded the way I felt: cranky, mean, and walking through my life with two left feet.

Kristy jumped right on it, not surprisingly. But to my amazement she opened with, "You know, I understand why you lied about being benched. It's something I might do."

"Really?" That stopped me in midpacking.

I should have known that Kristy wasn't about to let me off that easily.

"Yes," she said. "Really. Because being benched is something to be embarrassed about.

You don't get benched without good reason."

"Duh," I said as sarcastically as I could and concentrated on packing my bag again. Only this time I wasn't folding my clothes. I was cramming them in by the handful. I was angry.

Kristy rolled right over it. "Yeah. And I hate to say this, but you deserved to be benched. You were hogging the ball, you weren't listening to your coach, and you weren't working with your team. The fight wasn't even the worst part of it, in my opinion."

"Don't hold anything back, Kristy," I said, even more sarcastically. "Tell me how you really feel." I swung around to face her, my hands clenched.

"And you're a bad sport," added Kristy matter-of-factly. "Everything you did — that was being a bad sport. The fight only proved it."

I'd heard enough. "Thanks for your expert opinion," I snapped. I grabbed my bag and charged toward the door.

"You know it's true," said Kristy. "That's what's really making you angry. You know you were wrong and you won't admit it."

"Get out of my way." I pushed past Kristy and out the door, then thundered down the stairs. At the bottom I turned and shouted up, "Thanks for your hospitality."

After that, I went home to my family.

Did they welcome me with open arms? They

did, in spite of the fact that I probably had steam coming out of my ears. "Abby, darling," my mother said and gave me a big hug. We're not big on hugs and kisses, but at the moment, I welcomed it. I hugged her back, hard, and then I hugged Anna for good measure.

Anna smiled. "I guess you missed us, huh?"

"Maybe," I said.

"How did your game go?" Mom asked.

"Fine," I said. I tried to think of some way to tell the truth without lying about my role in the situation. "We won. But you were right. They could have won the game without me."

"You did what you had to do," said Mom (which made me feel worse).

I gulped. Then I said quickly, "Let me go put my stuff in my room."

"Hurry back and we'll tell you all about our visit," said Mom. "Grandmother and Grandfather send their love."

"Right," I muttered.

When I got to my room, I took my time unpacking. I smoothed out the wadded clothes that were clean. I took the dirty clothes to the laundry room. I wiped off my cleats (even though I hadn't used them) and put them in their place in the closet. I hung up my uniform on the back of my closet door to air out. (I didn't need to wash it because I hadn't played, so it wasn't dirty.)

I even started a load of laundry. Mom's head appeared around the edge of the laundry room door. "Oh, Abby. That's nice of you," she said. "But don't do that now. Come join us."

"On my way," I said. I dawdled for a few minutes longer, but it was no use. Sooner or later, I had to hear about the weekend my family had spent together on Long Island.

Without me.

Whoa. What was this? I'd chosen not to go. I gritted my teeth into a smile and went into the kitchen to join Anna and Mom over iced tea.

They'd had a good time. Our grandparents had prepared a Shabbat feast on Friday night. Everyone had gone to synagogue the next morning, and to visit Dad's grave on Sunday morning.

"We put flowers on it," said Anna. "The tree near him has gotten much bigger."

Mom said, "It's a very peaceful place. I'd never thought of it that way before. When it first happened . . . " Her voice trailed off, then she cleared her throat. "At first, after your father was killed, I hated the cemetery. I only took you girls there because I was supposed to. Everyone kept saying it would help you accept that your father was . . . gone."

"Well, it didn't," I said harshly. I knew well enough what my father's gravesite looked like. From my memories of those visits there, the cemetery was gray and full of shadows. The wind made a mournful sound. Everything tasted like salt from the tears that I couldn't cry.

Both Mom and Anna looked at me with so much sympathy that I wanted to cry then. But, of course, I didn't.

"Oh, Abby," said Mom, and she reached out as if she might hold my hand, just as she'd reached out in the restaurant. But this time I was ready. I pulled my hand back.

Anna, who as my twin probably knows more about how I am feeling than anyone else in the world, was less sympathetic. "You should have come," she said. "You know you should have."

It was too much. For the second time that afternoon, someone was telling me that I'd done something wrong, and that I knew it, and that I should have done things differently. When Kristy had done it, I had been angry.

But when Anna did it, it hurt.

I set my glass down gently. "Yes," I said. "Well, it's too late now, isn't it?"

"We'll go back sometime soon," Mom said. I could tell she was trying to intervene, trying to protect both Anna and me.

"Whatever," I said, with deliberate flippancy. "Now, if you'll excuse me, I have homework to do."

I picked up the glass again and took it to the

sink to rinse it out. Then I put it in the dish-washer. I could feel Anna and Mom watching me. They were still watching me when I walked out of the kitchen and closed the door softly behind me.

# CHAPTER 13

The Greenvale Lions were not as inexperienced as the Sheridan Stars had been. I could tell they were trouble from the moment they went into their warm-up routine on the other side of the field. They were totally engrossed in it, unrolling each drill as if it were a precision dance number, weaving in and out and playing as though the entire team were being controlled from some kind of central command.

I'm exaggerating, of course, but if their drills were any indication, they were a team that played well together "like a well-oiled machine," as the phrase goes.

I could tell that Coach Wu was reading the Lions the same way. She studied them intently, then made several sketches on her coach's board, erased those, and made several more, referring to her roster all the while.

For a moment, I allowed myself to hope. Surely Coach Wu would put me in today. I'd sat out the game against the Stars without a word of complaint. I'd come to practice and worked harder than I had ever worked in my life.

Harder because it was the most difficult thing I have ever had to do — stay in a defensive position and pass the ball out to the midfield and the front line, over and over again. I was itching to run in and take a shot at the goal. There were times when I could see the path between my feet and the goal as if it were drawn in fluorescent paint, from my toe to the back of the net.

But I didn't do it. I controlled myself. And, okay, I learned something about soccer that I had never known before. I learned to start looking at the field from a defensive point of view. It was an interesting perspective, one I'd never fully appreciated.

At the end of the last practice, Coach Wu had even said, "Good work, Abby."

Both Erin and I had been on the outside of our team looking in. But as time passed and we all practiced together, and since Erin and I were being scrupulously polite to each other when we couldn't avoid contact, our teammates had slipped back into the more easygoing give-and-take typical of a team.

So I hoped I would get to play against the Lions. Then I forced myself not to hope. Coach

Wu had said two games, and I didn't think she was the sort of person to change her mind.

The Booster Club had turned out in force and was putting its heart and soul into the pregame cheers. I knew that its enthusiasm was given an extra edge by the knowledge that Stacey had an envelope with the money the Club had raised from button sales and the car wash. According to Stacey's calculations, if we could find someone who would give us just a bit of a break on the Stoneybrook United shirts, and would do the job fast, we could have them by the next game.

I wondered if I would be wearing the shirt out on the field or still sitting on the bench.

The Greenvale Lions scored in the first five minutes of play, a tiny little tap off the outside of the left wing's foot into the corner of the goal just past Sandy's outstretched hands.

She lay in the dirt for a moment while the other team jumped for joy around the field. Then she scrambled up and retrieved the ball. She did not look happy. She made a face and gave the ball to the ref so play could resume.

The Lions scored twice more, both of the goals on the ground. Sandy stopped half a dozen other shots and barely missed the ones that went in. She got up, covered with more dirt and grass each time.

Then Jojo got the ball out of our defensive

end and sent it down the wing to Jeana, who wasted no time in moving it even further into their defensive end. Galvanized, the United players swarmed down the field after her. The Lions were just a step too slow in getting back, and a loose ball in front of the Lions' goal got converted to a score when Annalise did a sort of slide tackle into the ball and it squirted in.

The game became more evenly balanced after that, and the half ended 3–1 in favor of the Lions.

I think I expected our team to be talking about the fact that we were losing, but I was wrong. "Great saves," Jojo was exclaiming to Sandy.

"And your goal was awesome, Annalise," Sandy told our right wing.

"Once we got it out of our end of the field, we had to score," Annalise said happily.

Sandy said, "I'm playing okay, I think. But maybe Petra should be in the goal in my place second half."

Coach Wu stopped studying her clipboard to study Sandy's face. "What makes you say that?"

"Because Petra has done better in practice at catching the balls on the ground than I have," said Sandy. "And that's where they're scoring their goals."

"That's a good point," Coach Wu said. To Petra she said, "You'd better get warmed up for the second half."

"I'll warm you up," said Sandy, scooping up a soccer ball.

The team cheer as the halftime ended was a rousing one, heartily seconded by the Booster Club. I made it a point to look over at them and wave. But I pointedly ignored Kristy.

Not that she noticed. She seemed to be ignoring me too.

Oh, well. I could take it. Ignoring Abby was the latest pastime around Stoneybrook these days, I thought. Ignoring me and being angry with me.

We played better in the second half. Sandy's sacrifice was not in vain. Petra smothered every ground shot that came her way.

But we still weren't clearing the ball out of our defensive end so that we could go on the attack. I found myself sliding off the bench to pace the sidelines, studying the defense, trying to figure out what needed to be done.

*I could get that ball out,* I thought. *I could get it to the front line so they could score.*

Then I stopped in shock at what I was thinking. I was actually thinking like a defender.

At that moment I felt a hand on my shoulder. Coach Wu was standing beside me. Erin was with her.

"I'm putting you two in for the end of this half," she said abruptly. "Play like teammates, not like enemies, do you understand? Don't let yourselves down and *don't* let your team down."

I was so overjoyed that I would have promised anything. It was clear that Erin felt the same way. We were both still nodding like crazy, assuring Coach Wu that we would never play any other way when the ball went out of play and she signaled the referee that she wanted to sub us in.

I won't say we changed the flow of the game. But Erin got one goal and an assist on another. And she got that first goal because I nipped the ball away from the left wing and cleared it back up the field in two short, sweet moves — so fast that the Lions were caught flat-footed (or flat-pawed).

The game ended in a 3–3 tie.

It wasn't a win, but it wasn't a loss either. And I was off the bench.

"Nice game," I forced myself to mumble to Erin.

"Thanks," she said flatly.

I felt all the old anger returning. I was trying not to be a jerk, but she wasn't. "And you're a good sport too," I blurted out.

That stopped her. She pressed her lips together and we glared at each other. Then Erin suddenly said in a bright, cheerful voice, "Thank you," and moved away from me.

Coach Wu said, "Good work, Abby. I knew I was right about your ability to learn how to play defense."

"I'm good at offense too," I said. Since I was blurting things out, why stop now?

But Coach Wu only smiled. "I know. But there's a time and a place for everything. You'll see." She patted my shoulder.

So things were better with Coach Wu. But things were as bad as ever with Erin.

"We're going for pizza," Jojo called. "Want to come? The Booster Club is going with us."

Annalise said, "And they say they have a surprise for us. Coach is coming too."

These were temptations I could resist.

I envisioned sitting in the pizza parlor, while Kristy glared at me and everyone treated Erin like the Queen of the World. I shook my head. "No thanks," I said. "I've got to run."

I was telling the truth — literally. My brief time on the soccer field had barely been a warm-up for me. I was burning up with energy.

I waved at my team and the Booster Club in a vague way, then took off.

Fifteen minutes later I had stowed my gear

bag under a bench and was easing into a slow trot on the track at Miller's Park.

Miller's Park is beautiful and lies on the outskirts of Stoneybrook. People use it mostly to walk around and admire nature. From what I've heard, the town had a big fight with a local developer that ended with Miller's Park being declared an historic landmark so that it can't ever be developed or changed.

Fortunately, a small track had been put in long before it acquired landmark status. Other tracks are bigger and fancier and have more modern surfaces, but the Miller's Park track is at the edge of a field by a little hill, with trees around it. Flowers bloom in the middle of the track in the spring, and you can see rabbits playing there sometimes, just before dusk. The track even has a start and finish line. It's the same line, with START written in front of it and FINISH written behind it.

Kids are usually running around the nearby playground, their parents watching. The setting is peaceful.

Today only two families were at the playground swings and I had the track to myself. I took deep breaths of the cool air and tried to relax and fall into a comfortable pace. I knew that once I did, my mind would clear and then maybe, just maybe, I'd be able to think clearly

110

about all the things that had been happening.

*Slap, slap, slap.* I rounded the far end of the track — and almost fell over in shock.

Erin had just run out onto the other side of the oval. What was she doing here, at *my* track?

*Oh, great,* I thought. *She'll probably get me thrown off the track too.*

Well, I wasn't going to let her push me around anymore. Clenching my teeth, I ran by her.

Behind me, I heard her start to run. Before we had run very far, I realized that Erin was catching up with me.

I picked up my pace.

In a moment, my ears told me that Erin had picked up her pace too. She pulled even with me.

Staring straight ahead, I concentrated on keeping my stride smooth.

Erin passed me. It was too much. I kicked into the next gear and sped past her. For another half circuit of the track, I held the lead.

Then Erin passed me again. Her face was bright red. Her stride wasn't as smooth and even as it had been.

I sprinted. I gave it everything I had to pull even with Erin. We were running shoulder-to-shoulder, stride for stride. My own breath was coming in loud gasps and I knew hers was too.

We were approaching the finish line again. I resolved to beat Erin if it took the last breath in my body. I ran with all my might toward the finish line, but Erin matched me. We swept forward. The finish line came up to meet us and . . .

# CHAPTER 14

We crossed it at the same time.

And at the same time we swerved off into the grass. Erin ran to the outside of the track and I fell onto the middle.

I lay on my back with my arms over my head, sucking in air for all I was worth. I was wiped out. I felt as if I had run a marathon. For a moment, I even felt a little sick and giddy. But that passed.

Staring up at the sky through the lacework of leaves and branches, I realized that it was a perfect day. A perfect day for soccer, a perfect day for track.

A perfect day to stop being a jerk and blaming Erin for everything.

I sat up to find that Erin was already sitting up. She looked at me. We stared at each other for a long, long moment.

"What are you doing here?" I asked at last. "Why aren't you eating pizza with the team?"

113

"I didn't feel like it, I guess," Erin answered.

Another moment of silence followed. Then I said, "I want to apologize — "

At the same time, Erin said, "I'm sorry."

We stopped. I said, "I didn't mean to interrupt you or anything but I just wanted to say that I've been a big, stu — I mean, *super* jerk."

Erin grinned suddenly. "It's okay. You can call yourself a stupid jerk." Her grin disappeared. "But you shouldn't have called me stupid. You shouldn't call anybody stupid."

"You're right," I said. And as I said it, I realized how simple it was. It wasn't about who was smarter, or a better soccer player, or who had mental retardation. You didn't call anyone stupid or any other kind of derogatory name. "You're right," I repeated. "I shouldn't have called you stupid. I shouldn't call anyone stupid, ever."

Erin said, "Well, I shouldn't have punched at you like that."

"Yeah, you should save that kind of thing for the soccer game, when the referee isn't looking."

Erin's eyes widened, and I realized that it might take her awhile to get used to my sense of humor. But that was nothing new. I was used to being my own best audience for my jokes. "Just kidding," I said quickly.

"Oh." Erin thought it over, then smiled. "Yeah." Then she said, "Soccer is a good game. I'm a good player. Good as you are. Good enough to be center forward."

I swallowed hard on that one. It was true. But not getting to play what I thought of as "my" position still hurt.

On the other hand, it wasn't as if I had lost my spot to a bad player. I said, "Yeah. But you know, I miss it. Playing defense is — "

"All the work with none of the cheers," supplied Erin, wrinkling her nose.

"Yeah, mostly. Unless you've got an audience who really appreciates soccer. And where are you going to find that around here?"

Erin nodded. "I know."

We sat in silent contemplation of the unfairness of life and even of soccer, sometimes.

Then I said, "But it's kind of fun, taking the ball away from those show-off forwards and kicking it back down the field."

I shot a sly glance at Erin. She tipped her nose in the air and said, "You wish."

And laughed. I laughed too. I said, "I was a rotten sport, though, and I blamed you for everything, even though I was the one who was letting the team down and being a show-off and a ball hog."

Erin got to her feet, crossed the track, and

reached down to give me a hand up. "I let the team down too," she said. "You want to talk to Coach at practice?"

"I guess I could do that," I agreed.

Erin motioned toward the playground. "My family is here. Do you want a ride home?"

"Yes," I said. "Thank you. I'd like that."

I fell asleep faster that night and slept better than I had in a long time. But then I awoke suddenly, as if something were wrong.

Did I hear a strange noise? Was the house on fire? I tensed, listening and sniffing.

But the house remained still and calm and quiet. What had made me wake up like that?

I was about to roll over and force myself to go back to sleep when an image came into my mind.

Me, a much younger me. I was on a school bus, looking out the window. I saw my dad outside, standing on the sidewalk. I waved. He blew me a kiss.

That was the last time I had seen my dad before he was killed in a car wreck. I hadn't known I'd never see him again. But the bus had gone on, taking me to school and taking me away from him.

The next image was of Grandpa Morris, my mother's father, in the principal's office. He had tears in his eyes. Then Anna walked into the office.

116

Grandpa leaned over and put an arm around each of us. His voice cracked as he said, "There's been a car accident. Your father is . . . was . . . killed."

And that was when the world had stopped being safe and good.

My father was dead. I'd never even gotten to say good-bye.

I'd hated him for that, much as I'd loved him. Hated him for what he'd done to me, to us, to our family, by dying.

But of course, he hadn't done it to us. He hadn't meant to do it. He would never, ever have left us.

And he would always be my father. He would always charge through life with my energy, look back at me from the mirror with my eyes, make wonderful music with Anna's heart and hands.

I could say good-bye to what had been without losing him.

Tomorrow, I decided, I would tell Mom and Anna the truth. And then I would ask if we could go back to visit the cemetery in November on the anniversary of his death.

It would be an ending. But it would be a beginning too.

# CHAPTER 15

"So, had any good fights with neighbors lately?" I called to Kristy the next morning. She was shooting hoops in her driveway.

Kristy turned sharply. "Oh. Hi, Abby," she said. She looked a little wary. And also a little belligerent.

That's Kristy for you.

I smiled. Kristy sort of smiled back.

"Okay," I said. "Enough small talk. I'm sorry. I acted like a big, stupid jerk. Also a bad sport, a rotten team member, and a crummy soccer player."

Kristy's smile went from sort-of to genuine. "Whew. That about covers it, I guess."

"I can keep going if you'd like," I said. "But I'd prefer not to."

"Okay," said Kristy. "Apology accepted."

Just like that, it was over. Kristy takes things hard, but she doesn't carry a grudge.

"How did the pizza party go yesterday?" I

asked. "Did the Boosters have fun mingling with the team?"

"Well, we were definitely heroes when we presented the money for the shirts to the team. In fact, the term I heard repeatedly from both sides was 'awesome,' " Kristy said. "Also, we may have to start a soccer spin-off of Kristy's Krushers. Every one of the Booster Club kids has decided that he or she should be playing soccer."

"Hey, you're going to have to name *that* team after me," I said. I pretended to think a minute. Then I said, "How about 'Abby's Animals'?"

"Ha-ha," said Kristy.

"You don't like that? Well, how about Stevenson's Stompers? Or Abby's Gales. Get it?"

Kristy groaned. "Stop. Stop," she begged.

I grinned. "For you, Kristy," I said sweetly, "anything."

I was in a very good mood that morning. I had gotten up extra early to make coffee and I had taken Mom a cup to have in bed. She'd struggled up on one elbow to eye me sleepily. "What's the occasion?" she said.

"I'm sorry I was so awful about going to Long Island," I told her. And then I told her the whole story.

She sipped her coffee and listened without saying anything. When I had finished, she said very quietly, "Oh, Abby. If only I had known."

"Known what?" I said. "How could you know? I didn't even know. It was my fault."

"It was nobody's fault," my mother said. "I should have realized that just because I could accept the idea of your father's death didn't mean that you were ready to do that." She looked at me with a rueful expression. "You've always done things on your own schedule."

"I woke up this morning and remembered when Dad was killed," I said.

"I used to dream about it," said Mom. "About waking up and answering the phone that day. Sometimes I'd dream that the voice at the other end said, 'There's been an accident, but everything's okay.' But I don't dream that dream anymore."

"I miss him," I said. "I guess I always will."

"Yes," said my mother.

"It hurts. I guess that won't go away either."

"I don't know," my mother said simply.

I took a deep breath. I said, "When we go back to Long Island, I have something I want to take to the cemetery for Dad."

I had an idea. I wanted to wait until after our last game to put it into effect, though.

We lost our last game, 2–1. But there were some victories too. I stayed in my new position. I did a good job. And the one goal we scored was off a long ball that I sent up the field. Petra trapped it and passed it neatly to Erin, who calmly put it away.

We also wore our brand-new purple shirts. After the game, Claudia took our team picture. She was going to have it enlarged and let everybody order copies. I planned on asking all my teammates to autograph my copy. Then I was going to put it on the wall with my posters of famous women athletes.

After the game, my team went to Pizza Express. To my surprise, several people (teammates and a couple of employees at Pizza Express) told me how great it was that I had friends who supported my team.

I'd never thought about it like that, but it was true. My friends had shown up to support me and the team I played on. And they proved to be true-blue because they'd kept on supporting the team even when I had acted like anything but a team player.

My friends and I were blowing bubbles in our drinks and talking soccer, soccer, soccer. They were making silly mustaches with their straws and trading the toppings from the pizza.

They were acting like a team. Like my team. I'd earned my place on it at last. It had been humbling, but humbling is okay sometimes. I had learned some important lessons.

I slurped some soda and scarfed some pizza

and felt generally right with the world. I thought about the new soccer cleats I was going to buy with the baby-sitting money I was saving.

You can't hold onto the past forever. It was time to let my lucky cleats go. When I visited my father's grave, I was going to knot the laces together and hang the cleats on one side of the stone.

And then I was going to tell him a little bit about who I'd become, about how far my old cleats had brought me, and where I hoped my life — and my new cleats — would take me.

I figured my father would like that.

# FIND OUT MORE ABOUT
# SPECIAL OLYMPICS AND
# UNIFIED SPORTS!

Special Olympics Unified Sports® provides opportunities for individuals with and without mental retardation to train and compete together on the same teams. There are 23 winter and summer sports to choose from! Teams are constructed to provide sports opportunities that meaningfully challenge all participants and often lead to improved self-esteem, equal status with peers, and new friendships. Special Olympics is truly "training for life"!

To find out how you can become involved in Special Olympics or compete on a Special Olympics Unified Sports® team, contact your local Special Olympics office, listed in the telephone book. Or check out Special Olympics on the Internet! (*http://www.specialolympics.org*)

Dear Reader,

For a long time, I've been interested in the Special Olympics. Special Olympics is a year-round program for people with mental retardation. Athletes train and compete in twenty-three official Special Olympics sports, including alpine and cross-country skiing, aquatics, basketball, bowling, figure skating, gymnastics, roller skating, soccer, softball, and track and field.

It is often said that Special Olympics is "training for life." The men, women, boys, and girls who train throughout the year are not only preparing themselves for competition but also for greater participation in family, work, school, and community life. Like Abby, participants in the Special Olympics Unified Sports® program learn a lot about teamwork, friendship, and spirit. It's an experience Abby will never forget!

To find out more about Special Olympics and Unified Sports, contact your local Special Olympics office (listed in the phone book) or check out the Special Olympics website at *http://www.specialolympics.org*.

Happy reading,

*Ann M Martin*

# Ann M. Martin

# About the Author

ANN MATTHEWS MARTIN was born on August 12, 1955. She grew up in Princeton, NJ, with her parents and her younger sister, Jane.

Although Ann used to be a teacher and then an editor of children's books, she's now a full-time writer. She gets ideas for her books from many different places. Some are based on personal experiences. Others are based on childhood memories and feelings. Many are written about contemporary problems or events.

All of Ann's characters, even the members of the Baby-sitters Club, are made up. (So is Stoneybrook.) But many of her characters are based on real people. Sometimes Ann names her characters after people she knows; other times she chooses names she likes.

In addition to the Baby-sitters Club books, Ann Martin has written many other books for children. Her favorite is *Ten Kids, No Pets* because she loves big families and she loves animals. Her favorite Baby-sitters Club book is *Kristy's Big Day*. (By the way, Kristy is her favorite baby-sitter!)

Ann M. Martin now lives in New York with her cats, Gussie and Woody. Her hobbies are reading, sewing, and needlework — especially making clothes for children.

# THE BABY SITTERS CLUB

## Notebook Pages

This Baby-sitters Club book belongs to _____.

I am _____ years old and in the _____

grade.

The name of my school is _____.

I got this BSC book from _____.

I started reading it on _____ and

finished reading it on _____.

The place where I read most of this book is _____.

My favorite part was when _____.

If I could change anything in the story, it might be the part when

_____.

My favorite character in the Baby-sitters Club is _____.

The BSC member I am most like is _____

because _____.

If I could write a Baby-sitters Club book it would be about _____

_____.

# #110 Abby the Bad Sport

Abby loves to play soccer. My favorite sport is _____

_____. The position I usually

play is _____

_____· I like/dislike this position because _____

_____

_____· Abby is benched after she fights with her

teammate Erin. The biggest problem I ever had with a teammate

was _____

_____

_____· Abby learns that it's no fun to be a bad sport. I think

bad sports are _____

_____· When I'm playing on a team, I always

make sure to _____

_____

_____· Abby's soccer team is named Stoneybrook

United. If I were naming a team in Stoneybrook, I would call it

_____.

Read all the books
about **Abby**
in the Baby-sitters Club series
by Ann M. Martin

# THE BABY-SITTERS CLUB

Look for #111

## STACEY'S SECRET FRIEND

Tess realized I was studying her outfit. "Like it?" she asked. "It was my mother's."

At least that answered the question of where she'd found it.

"I don't know," I said. I didn't want to be a hypocrite and say I adored it. "It's hard to get used to the style."

"I know," Tess beamed. "That's why I like it so much."

I nodded. "Well . . ." I let my voice trail off helplessly.

"Hey, want to come to my house tomorrow afternoon?" Tess asked. "I've got some books on castles. I dug up some photos I have, too. We could start on our project."

"I suppose so," I agreed. "Sure."

Tess smiled, then turned to open her locker. " 'Bye," I said, drifting away from her. I took one last look at her in that terrible plaid polyester pant suit and shivered with disbelief as I walked away.

The wheels in my head turned. I suddenly had a brilliant idea! Tomorrow I'd be alone with Tess. I could use the opportunity to give Tess a beauty makeover. This girl desperately needed to be saved from herself!

"Hey, Tess," I called to her. She stopped and turned toward me. "Do you mind if we work at my house. I . . . uh . . . have a BSC meeting and I can work longer if I'm not too far away." (This happened to be true, and was a convenient excuse.)

"Okay." Tess agreed.

I smiled and waved. Great! I had a day to plan Operation Makeover Tess.

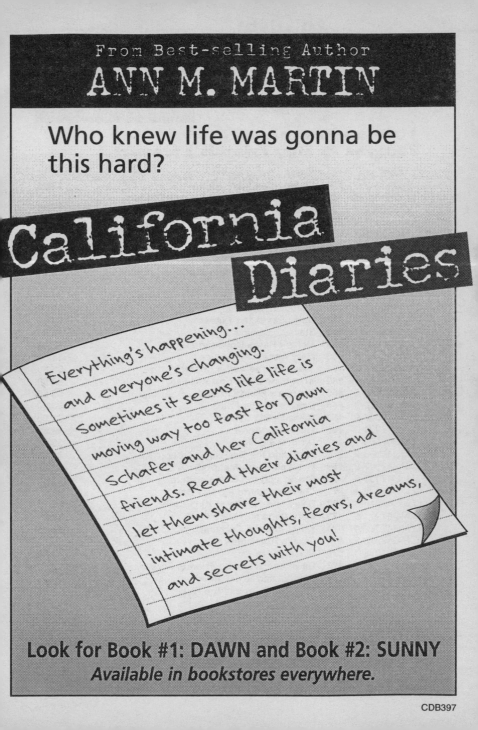

From Best-selling Author
# ANN M. MARTIN

Who knew life was gonna be this hard?

## California Diaries

Everything's happening... and everyone's changing. Sometimes it seems like life is moving way too fast for Dawn Schafer and her California friends. Read their diaries and let them share their most intimate thoughts, fears, dreams, and secrets with you!

**Look for Book #1: DAWN and Book #2: SUNNY**
*Available in bookstores everywhere.*

# THE BABY-SITTERS CLUB®

**Collect 'em all!**

## 100 (and more)
## Reasons to Stay Friends Forever!

*More titles...* ▶

| | | | |
|---|---|---|---|
| ❏ MG22872-2 | #88 | Farewell, Dawn | $3.50 |
| ❏ MG22873-0 | #89 | Kristy and the Dirty Diapers | $3.50 |
| ❏ MG22874-9 | #90 | Welcome to the BSC, Abby | $3.99 |
| ❏ MG22875-1 | #91 | Claudia and the First Thanksgiving | $3.50 |
| ❏ MG22876-5 | #92 | Mallory's Christmas Wish | $3.50 |
| ❏ MG22877-3 | #93 | Mary Anne and the Memory Garden | $3.99 |
| ❏ MG22878-1 | #94 | Stacey McGill, Super Sitter | $3.99 |
| ❏ MG22879-X | #95 | Kristy + Bart = ? | $3.99 |
| ❏ MG22880-3 | #96 | Abby's Lucky Thirteen | $3.99 |
| ❏ MG22881-1 | #97 | Claudia and the World's Cutest Baby | $3.99 |
| ❏ MG22882-X | #98 | Dawn and Too Many Sitters | $3.99 |
| ❏ MG69205-4 | #99 | Stacey's Broken Heart | $3.99 |
| ❏ MG69206 2 | #100 | Kristy's Worst Idea | $3.99 |
| ❏ MG69207-0 | #101 | Claudia Kishi, Middle School Dropout | $3.99 |
| ❏ MG69208-9 | #102 | Mary Anne and the Little Princess | $3.99 |
| ❏ MG69209-7 | #103 | Happy Holidays, Jessi | $3.99 |
| ❏ MG69210-0 | #104 | Abby's Twin | $3.99 |
| ❏ MG69211-9 | #105 | Stacey the Math Whiz | $3.99 |
| ❏ MG69212-7 | #106 | Claudia, Queen of the Seventh Grade | $3.99 |
| ❏ MG69213-5 | #107 | Mind Your Own Business, Kristy! | $3.99 |
| ❏ MG69214-3 | #108 | Don't Give Up, Mallory | $3.99 |
| ❏ MG69215-1 | #109 | Mary Anne to the Rescue | $3.99 |
| ❏ MG45575-3 | | Logan's Story Special Edition Readers' Request | $3.25 |
| ❏ MG47118-X | | Logan Bruno, Boy Baby-sitter | |
| | | Special Edition Readers' Request | $3.50 |
| ❏ MG47756-0 | | Shannon's Story Special Edition | $3.50 |
| ❏ MG47686-6 | | The Baby-sitters Club Guide to Baby-sitting | $3.25 |
| ❏ MG47314-X | | The Baby-sitters Club Trivia and Puzzle Fun Book | $2.50 |
| ❏ MG48400-1 | | BSC Portrait Collection: Claudia's Book | $3.50 |
| ❏ MG22864-1 | | BSC Portrait Collection: Dawn's Book | $3.50 |
| ❏ MG69181-3 | | BSC Portrait Collection: Kristy's Book | $3.99 |
| ❏ MG22865-X | | BSC Portrait Collection: Mary Anne's Book | $3.99 |
| ❏ MG48399-4 | | BSC Portrait Collection: Stacey's Book | $3.50 |
| ❏ MG92713-2 | | The Complete Guide to The Baby-sitters Club | $4.95 |
| ❏ MG47151-1 | | The Baby-sitters Club Chain Letter | $14.95 |
| ❏ MG48295-5 | | The Baby-sitters Club Secret Santa | $14.95 |
| ❏ MG45074-3 | | The Baby-sitters Club Notebook | $2.50 |
| ❏ MG44783-1 | | The Baby-sitters Club Postcard Book | $4.95 |

**Available wherever you buy books...or use this order form.**

---

**Scholastic Inc., P.O. Box 7502, 2931 E. McCarty Street, Jefferson City, MO 65102**

Please send me the books I have checked above. I am enclosing $_____
(please add $2.00 to cover shipping and handling). Send check or money order–
no cash or C.O.D.s please.

Name _____ Birthdate_____

Address _____

City_____ State/Zip _____

BSC1196

## by Ann M. Martin

**Collect and read these exciting BSC Super Specials, Mysteries, and Super Mysteries along with your favorite Baby-sitters Club books!**

### BSC Super Specials

### BSC Mysteries

**More titles ➡**

## The Baby-sitters Club books continued...

| | | |
|---|---|---|
| ❏ BAI47050-7 | #12 Dawn and the Surfer Ghost | $3.50 |
| ❏ BAI47051-5 | #13 Mary Anne and the Library Mystery | $3.50 |
| ❏ BAI47052-3 | #14 Stacey and the Mystery at the Mall | $3.50 |
| ❏ BAI47053-1 | #15 Kristy and the Vampires | $3.50 |
| ❏ BAI47054-X | #16 Claudia and the Clue in the Photograph | $3.99 |
| ❏ BAI48232-7 | #17 Dawn and the Halloween Mystery | $3.50 |
| ❏ BAI48233-5 | #18 Stacey and the Mystery at the Empty House | $3.50 |
| ❏ BAI48234-3 | #19 Kristy and the Missing Fortune | $3.50 |
| ❏ BAI48309-9 | #20 Mary Anne and the Zoo Mystery | $3.50 |
| ❏ BAI48310-2 | #21 Claudia and the Recipe for Danger | $3.50 |
| ❏ BAI22866-8 | #22 Stacey and the Haunted Masquerade | $3.50 |
| ❏ BAI22867-6 | #23 Abby and the Secret Society | $3.99 |
| ❏ BAI22868-4 | #24 Mary Anne and the Silent Witness | $3.99 |
| ❏ BAI22869-2 | #25 Kristy and the Middle School Vandal | $3.99 |
| ❏ BAI22870-6 | #26 Dawn Schafer, Undercover Baby-sitter | $3.99 |
| ❏ BAI69175-9 | #27 Claudia and the Lighthouse Ghost | $3.99 |
| ❏ BAI69176-7 | #28 Abby and the Mystery Baby | $3.99 |
| ❏ BAI69177-5 | #29 Stacey and the Fashion Victim | $3.99 |
| ❏ BAI69178-3 | #30 Kristy and the Mystery Train | $3.99 |

## BSC Super Mysteries

| | | |
|---|---|---|
| ❏ BAI48311-0 | Baby-sitters' Haunted House  Super Mystery #1 | $3.99 |
| ❏ BAI22871-4 | Baby-sitters Beware  Super Mystery #2 | $3.99 |
| ❏ BAI69180-5 | Baby-sitters' Fright Night  Super Mystery #3 | $4.50 |

---

### Available wherever you buy books...or use this order form.

**Scholastic Inc., P.O. Box 7502, 2931 East McCarty Street, Jefferson City, MO 65102-7502**

Please send me the books I have checked above. I am enclosing $ _____
(please add $2.00 to cover shipping and handling). Send check or money order
— no cash or C.O.D.s please.

Name_____Birthdate_____

Address _____

City_____State/Zip_____

Please allow four to six weeks for delivery. Offer good in the U.S. only. Sorry, mail orders are not
available to residents of Canada. Prices subject to change.

BSCM1196